THE RETURN

He had "victim" written all over him...

While searching for buried treasure Michael Jolly finds bones and a skull. In the hope of a reward Jolly calls the police and soon finds Chief Inspector Hennessey and Sergeant Yellich appear on the scene of this decades-old crime. Meanwhile, Margaret South – devoted wife and magistrate – is haunted by the unlovable face of Norris Smith ... Whatever did happen to him that unnervingly quiet night?

THE RETURN

THE RETURN

Peter Turnbull

Severn House Large Print
London & New York

This first large print edition published in Great Britain 2002 by
SEVERN HOUSE LARGE PRINT BOOKS LTD of
9-15, High Street, Sutton, Surrey, SM1 1DF.
First world regular print edition published 2001 by
Severn House Publishers, London and New York.
This first large print edition published in the USA 2002 by
SEVERN HOUSE PUBLISHERS INC., of
595 Madison Avenue, New York, NY 10022

LINCOLNSHIRE
COUNTY COUNCIL

British Library Cataloguing in Publication Data

Turnbull, Peter, 1950 -
    The return. - Large print ed.
    1. Hennessey, Chief Inspector (Fictitious character) - Fiction
    2. Yellich, Sergeant (Fictitious character) - Fiction
    3. Police - England - Yorkshire - Fiction
    4. Detective and mystery stories
    5. Large type books
    I. Title
    823.9'14 [F]

ISBN 0-7278-7197-8

Printed and bound in Great Britain by
MPG Books Ltd, Bodmin, Cornwall.

One

In which a lonely man makes a disturbing find, and in which a fulfilled woman finds it strange to feel a most profound sense of relief.

MONDAY

Michael Jolly felt the irony and the inappropriateness of his name and he felt it deeply. He felt it so because he felt himself to be a most lonely man, often telling himself that he was the loneliest of the lonely. Of all the lonely people, he was the loneliest. In this city of one hundred and seventy-five thousand persons there was not a single soul who would extend a hand of friendship.

He had been the only child of elderly parents who had doted upon him, lavished much upon him, praised him for every success, no matter how small, and always gave him whatever he wanted. They died leaving

7

him all alone in the world, and he now occupied the little terraced house in East Mount Road, near the railway station where he had lived with his parents. He was not happy to have visitors because there was no one to clean up for him and no one to cook for him, so the house was, he conceded, 'a bit of a mess' like a massive receptacle for Chinese takeaway meal dishes; and he also noticed that when people did call, like the man to read the gas meter, and the man who read the electricity meter, they seemed to want to leave quickly and he noticed how even the Seventh Day Adventists didn't try hard to save him but with their noses twitching would push a leaflet into his hands and move on down the terrace.

He would go out in the evenings to the pubs on Blossom Street or Micklegate Bar but people didn't want to talk to him no matter how hard he'd try to force a conversation – even after brushing his hair and putting on a tie, they still wouldn't speak to him. Usually they ignored him, sometimes they'd walk away to another part of the bar, sometimes they'd tell him to 'push off' in the brusque manner of Yorkshire people. Even offering to buy them a drink didn't work, in fact it often made it worse. Often the threat of violence was the reaction to his walking up to a stranger and offering to buy him a drink and Michael Jolly could never understand why. He was, after all, only trying to be nice, like his mummy had told him to be. 'Be nice, Michael,' her voice still hummed musically in his ears. 'Be nice and the world will be nice to you.' School didn't teach him anything. It taught others of his social class something, and some even went on to university and became lawyers or doctors, but it didn't do much for him, school didn't, even though he sat in front of books for hours on end. Nothing went in for him and they wouldn't give him any qualifications, but his mummy said not to worry, 'You'll just have to be nice and get along that way.'

Michael Jolly tore angrily at the packaging.

He'd taken a succession of jobs, all menial because that's all that he was offered. Sometimes he kept a job for a day and a half but left when he couldn't make people like him, even though he was being as nice as nice could be. Other times he kept a job for a few months and learned that the more solitary the occupation, the longer he kept the job – twelve months once. Often there would be long periods of unemployment during which he was prone to lying in bed all day, especially in the winter, because there was no reason to get up. He had now come to the end of one such period of employment as a cleaner at the hospital and he'd been sacked for stealing a little bit of money. But he'd really stolen more than they knew, and with it he'd bought a metal detector.

He had bought a metal detector because he had read on more than one occasion how people with such machines had uncovered buried treasure and had become rich. If he could find treasure he'd be rich and people would like him. And then, at the age of thirty-seven, he'd have a friend, more than one even. And maybe someone to cook and clean for him.

He surveyed the detector, a long handle attached to a hoop of metal, earphones, and an on/off switch. He switched it on and passed the hoop over a tinfoil tray which had contained last night's prawn fried rice and heard the high-pitched whine in his ears which subsided to silence as the hoop passed over the carpet. All he had to do now was to find some treasure. He glanced at the clock which had been his father's long service gift from the dairy, awarded to Len Jolly for thirty-five years' service with York and District Dairies. Thirty-five years a milkman. His mother had polished the brass

10

plate under the clock's face but he hadn't kept up the practice and the inscription was now barely legible. But so long as the clock kept good time, which it did, he wound it once each week, that was all that was necessary, so long as he could see the face, he didn't need to read the legend. And the clock told him that it was ten o'clock, and he knew it to be the forenoon, and outside he saw the weather was sunny and warm. It was after all the sixth month of the year.

Carrying his new possession, Michael Jolly walked away from his house with short, hurried steps, and took a cream single-decker 'Rider York' bus out into the country. With no carefully planned destination, he took a bus out to Stamford Bridge because he had once read of a battle that had taken place there. At Stamford Bridge, he walked out of the village until he was in open country. Flat, open country, fields of golden wheat and brilliant yellow oil seed, interspersed with an occasional stand of trees, ranging in size from copses to a large wood, and it was one such wood that attracted him. Set close to the road, so he didn't have to walk far, but at the end of a narrow almost grassed-over track which didn't look well or often used, with luck, he thought, with luck, he would be the first to 'detect'

11

the wood. As he neared the wood he saw a faded sign nailed to a tree which read 'Private Wood – Keep Out'. That encouraged him.

A private wood, not policed because the sign would not be so faded, but it might be sufficient to keep out other detectors. There really was, he thought, a good chance that he was to be the first to detect the wood, and to dig up a cache of coins that had lain buried for centuries or a sword with a handle and scabbard impregnated with diamonds and rubies and gold.

He stepped into the shade of the wood, brushing off flies which had gathered under the canopy of the trees. He began to 'detect', sweeping the instrument from side to side as he walked slowly and carefully between the trees. Another man might perhaps have enjoyed the wood for what it was, the rich foliage, the birdsong, the tranquillity, the mysticism, but Michael Jolly's thoughts were focused only on one thing, the sudden high-pitched whine in the earphones which might, just might, mean that he'd found a fortune. He continued to sweep, passed a stand of brambles, which to him seemed ripe for a well-placed fire to stimulate new growth, and came upon a small clearing, a sudden space in the wood's floor, about twice the size of the ground floor of his terraced house, and which was covered with a velvety carpet of moss.

The find, when it came, came soon after he entered the clearing. Just two paces into the clearing and the earphones began to screech. He switched off the detector and laid it to one side and took the trowel from his knapsack and began to dig. He dug furiously, noticing but not savouring the smell of newly turned soil as it rose to fill his nostrils. The trowel was not up to the job and so he lay it beside the detector and took the entrenching tool he'd bought at a car boot sale on York racecourse some months ago, slid the wooden handle into the opening above the blade and began to hack at the soil. He'd dug down just six or eight inches when he came across a tobacco tin, which he picked up and stared at in dismay. He held it, prising it open with the blade of the trowel and found it contained cigarette rolling apparatus, a packet of papers, remnants of tobacco and a shrivelled leaf of a vegetable.

Had Michael Jolly been a more curious man he might perhaps have pondered why anyone would want to bury such an item containing such ordinary contents? Yet buried it had been, the design of cigarette rolling apparatus which was no more than thirty years old would have dated it for him, and he might have known that the tin could not have worked itself so deeply into the soil in that time. But such thoughts and points of observation did not occur to Michael Jolly. The tobacco tin wasn't treasure and so he replaced the lid and tossed the tin contemptuously to the side of the clearing.

He turned at the sound of a motor vehicle and watched a John Deere being driven at speed along the country road. He saw the driver clearly, a young man, stripped to the waist, but being concealed by the woods, the driver of the tractor didn't see Michael Jolly. Jolly turned back and picked up the detector, switched it on, and scanned the hole. Again the earphones made a high-pitched whine. There was more metal beneath where the tobacco tin had been. He laid the detector on the ground, picked up the entrenching tool and once again hacked at the ground.

A pair of spectacles.

A metal-framed rucksack, containing clothing, all now rotten and which crumbled at the slightest touch.

A bone, attached to another bone attached to a skull. A human skull.

Michael Jolly stood back from the shallow

grave he had discovered, and uncovered. Slowly his face, which was expressionless, slowly broke into a smile. He cared not for the person in the ground, whoever he or she had been, they were now long past caring. He didn't care that the find was not a hoard of gold coins buried in ancient times, because this find meant money as well. It had to. There'd be a reward, people offer money for information leading to the whereabouts of missing persons and he'd found a missing person. All now bone, but he'd found him. Or her. And if there was no reward in this case, then he had a story to sell, newspapers pay good money, really serious money for stories like this, not the local ones, but the national Sundays, especially if this bundle of bones had once been a famous person, or had been linked to a big crime. He felt elated, him in the green wood, a hole, bones in the hole ... life was going to be nice to him after all. Mummy had been right all along.

Margaret South had, up until the April of that year, considered herself a fortunate and, above all, a fulfilled, woman. She was in her forties, with still nearly eight years to go before the big 'Five-O'. She had three children, all now late teenagers, all doing well with their studies, each with eyes on a university place and a career in one of the professions. Her husband was a doctor, a family GP, she was a lay magistrate and also gave time to the charity shop in Knaresborough, and also to the Citizen's Advice Bureau in the town, where she and her family lived, prestigiously, in a large house in Lands Lane. It was then, just when everything was going so well, so smoothly, that the memory returned.

Margaret South had read of the concept of 'recovered memory', and she had also read of the 'false memory syndrome' and of the debate between 'real' and 'false' memory, though she had not come down on one side or the other. The debate didn't affect her, it was of no more than passing interest. It had really been a 'buzz' in the closing years of the previous century, of instances of costly legal battles in the United States where the issue of the accuracy or falsehood of a person's memory was put to the test, often with the prospect of long-term imprisonment for the accused and vindication of the accuser being at issue, though so far as Margaret South could see, the only real beneficiaries were, as always, the lawyers, who trousered huge fees. The issue became focused for her when she recovered the memory.

She remembered the moment precisely. It was on a bracing day. She walked from her home into Knaresborough. On her right was a series of expensive homes, much like her own, and to her left was the rich soil of a newly ploughed field, a stand of swaying trees with crows cawing against a vast blue sky. She even remembered that there had been a vapour trail of a jet plane, high above, twin streaks of white against the light blue vastness. For then, at that moment, there was the sensation of an impact in her stomach, and the sounds about her, the traffic, the crows, became louder, the colours became brighter, sharper somehow, details she had never noticed became noticed as her powers of observation became instantly enhanced as if a voice said to her 'This is Life,' loudly. Very loudly ... 'And it can be taken away from you'. Because suddenly, with no discernible trigger, in the space of taking three paces she recovered the memory of the death of Norris Smith. And not just his death, but his murder, and not just his murder, but the part she had played in it.

She was a conspirator to murder. She, a magistrate, an adviser at the CAB, a helper in the charity shop, the wife of a general practitioner, the mother of three beautiful, intelligent children, destined for the professions; she was all these, she had that responsibility to live up to. And she was also a conspirator to murder. And now all could be taken from her, probably would be, her betrayal of her family, her betrayal of the Knaresborough Bench, she had sent people to prison, and she ... she had stopped walking, stopped in her tracks.

Dead in her tracks.

Just stood there, staring into space with the sensation that she was no longer on a firm footing, that there was no longer anything beneath her, not even a safety net. Then she had gathered herself, collected herself, and continued to walk into the town. But she was a changed woman. That evening she was unable to conceal her emotions and fended off solicitous concern from her husband with platitudes such as 'It's all right, it's just a headache ... I'll have an early night'. The following day she had phoned the CAB to tell them she would not be coming in – she 'had a migraine' – and had collected the family dog, and taken her car, and had driven to the wood.

She could recall the approximate location of the wood, outside York, near Stamford Bridge, between Stamford Bridge and Full

Sutton where the prison was.

The Prison. That word had suddenly come to have a new resonance for her. It was no longer a place where other people go.

But the big house had been near Full Sutton. They had done the journey in daylight hours, dusk really, but summer dusk, natural light enough to see the route they were taking on Bernard's instructions, she and Paul in the front, Bernard too in the front and Norris ... Norris's body in the rear. Going along with Bernard, doing what he said, they had arrived at the wood, driving over a field to get to it, and as the two men dug the grave she had collected Norris's things from the rear of the Land Rover, his inexpensive red rucksack, his pathetic working-class tobacco tin ... What did he call it? His 'self-contained snout tin', that was it. If nothing else, she had learned from Norris that in Yorkshire working-class culture a cigarette is sometimes known as a 'snout'.

She recalled how she had watched Norris's body, so small compared to Bernard's massive build, being rolled into the hole, how the rucksack had been taken from her and put on top of his body and how she had tossed the 'snout tin' in after the rucksack. She remembered how Bernard had rummaged in the edge of the clearing and had returned with moss, both hands full of moss, which he laid on the filled-in grave. 'Soon grow,' he'd said. Then he added, 'Don't worry, it's a private wood, nobody will come into it and he's down too far for the foxes to dig him up.' They had then driven back over the field, over a ditch which jolted the Land Rover violently and had gone back to the big house and whisky. Too much whisky.

The next day, she and Paul Stapylton had driven back to York in his Land Rover, the ex-ministry vehicle he called 'The Green Goddess'. She remembered how they didn't speak during the journey, how he dropped her at York Railway Station, across the road from the station, close to the cholera graves beneath the wall, how she had swivelled herself out of the passenger seat of the Land Rover clutching her holdall, and stepped on to the grass verge, closing the door behind her, not saying anything at all to Paul Stapylton nor even glancing at him, sensing that he was not even looking at her. They had done something, each reminded the other of it, so they didn't look at each other. Looking back it was, she realised, the beginning of another burial, this time it was the burial of the memory. The timing had helped, she later realised. It had been the summer after their finals, during which group members had gone their separate ways and she never saw Bernard or Paul Stapylton again. She had difficulty even remembering their faces, as if some strong force in her mind was blocking out all trace of that period of her life. If you can't remember what someone looks like, she had once read, the trick is to remember them in a specific context, in a pub, on a walk, in a restaurant, in the sitting-room of the house ... but there was no context of her days at university she could use to remember her friends.

She had got on with life, became a wife, became a mother, and became fulfilled and emotionally wealthy and, as the wife of a GP, money had been, well ... sufficient. And her life was good. It was good until one afternoon in April when she had walked from her home the short distance into Knaresborough during which, as if turning on some subconscious impulse, her mind had recovered *the* memory. Her scalp had crawled, a chill had shot down her spine, her stomach following a sense of impact then had seemed hollow, because twenty-plus years earlier she had been party to a murder. Her memory of it had not been erased, but buried, and what is buried tends to work its way to the surface. No ... she thought as she stood there, stock-still, no, they don't tend to work their way to the surface, memories don't tend to do anything of the sort. They *do* surface and surface clearly. Eventually.

Drawn with guilt, drawn with horrific, dark fascination, as murderers are reputed to return to the scene of their crime, so Margaret South returned to the wood; by finding the big house, she picked up the dread route they had taken years earlier in the Green Goddess and had eventually found it. Set back from the road, one field distant, it was, she thought, about quarter of a mile square. She parked the car close to the path which led to the wood and, taking 'Silver' the spaniel with her, walked into the wood for the first time in more than twenty years one day after a rainfall which had sharpened the smell of the vegetation and soil.

To an observer, it was a privileged middle-aged lady of slender figure, wrapped in a Burberry and hat and scarf, taking her pedigree dog for a short walk across brown fields to a green wood under a wide, blustery grey sky, having first parked her compact red Mercedes 190 by the side of the road. But

22

the observer would not know of the torment within the mind of the lady, and that she felt anything but privileged.

In the wood, Margaret South found the clearing rapidly and saw that in the years that had elapsed the two handfuls of moss that Bernard Ffyrst had placed over Norris's unmarked and shallow grave had grown to carpet the clearing. She stood at the edge of the clearing and, unable to control herself, wept bitterly and said, 'Oh, Norris ... I'm so sorry, so very sorry ... what did we do to you?'

Thereafter she had continued to visit the wood and to stand beside, but never ever on the spot, where Norris lay. She had had respect for him and she did like him, she did, really she did. It couldn't have been easy for him, with Bernard Ffyrst and Paul Stapylton. Their cutting remarks, insulting by innuendo with their ex-public schoolboy ways ... and she had done the same, but she was young, still learning, and Norris was ... well he was just such a target.

Now she felt so guilty, so ashamed, so guilty, not just for Norris who, as she had once read engraved on a Victorian gravestone, had been 'cut off in the bud of life', but for the betrayal of her family – her children who had not yet been born – because they would soon find out that their mother was a murderer.

So April had given way to May and she, having resigned from the bench and the CAB no longer feeling able to work even at the charity shop, had taken to making frequent visits to Norris's grave. Not daily visits, that was not feasible, but twice or three times, midweek, when the children were at college and her husband in his surgery or on his rounds. Although such was her all-consuming guilt that she had on one Saturday afternoon, and on one Sunday after the ten a.m. communion service, stolen away to visit the wood and the clearing within the wood. Church, the Anglican community to which she belonged, that part was difficult, it was the worst in fact. The communion wafer seemed to choke her, the wine tasted so bitter ... but she had to go, to refuse would bring on questions from her family, particularly from her husband, with his soft voice. 'No ... now come on, that's not the answer. What is the answer? Don't evade, don't side-step...' Such questioning to one to whom she had made vows which she intended to keep and with whom she had made a mutual 'no secrets pact' she could not handle, not yet, she was not ready for such questions. She also wanted to tell him rather than give in to questions, giving in to questions was no way for this horrible secret to come out. So she had maintained a normal day-to-day life-style so far as she could, but she was a woman who wore her emotion on her sleeve and her husband would say, on occasion, 'You know, one day you're going to tell me what's bothering you.' But she needed time to think, above all she needed time to think, so in response she would smile and say, 'Nothing's bothering me, promise.'

Michael Jolly was for once in his life, jolly by nature. He packed up the entrenching tool and trowel in his knapsack and picked up the metal detector, walked out and away from the wood with short, hurried steps and then broke into a run, running as he had always run, and for which he had been ridiculed by his peers when at school, kicking his legs out straight and at forty-five degrees to each other. He ran to the road and on to Stamford Bridge, running as fast as he could, motivated by the money that the newspapers would pay for his story, so he made it good, running to raise the alarm would make a better read one Sunday from now for a few people down the pub. He reached Stamford Bridge, it was quiet, with few people around. He saw a phone box and went to it, and dialled 999. He deserved it, he thought, as his call was snappily answered, he deserved a break in his life.

George Hennessey disliked driving. He did in fact detest it, and he detested it for deeply personal reasons which he rarely spoke about, but because of which he could never fathom humankind's love affair with the most dangerous machine ever invented. But occasionally, and this was one such occasion, he had to drive, there was no other means of completing the journey. He drove from York out to Stamford Bridge, the lush countryside of the Vale, the distant skyline, the big sky, isolated cottages and narrow lanes going off the main road. It would be, he thought, a pleasant drive for anyone who liked driving.

From Stamford Bridge he followed the directions that he had been given over the phone by Sergeant Yellich whose voice seemed to Hennessey to have had a curious mixture of calm and control, together with an excitement. The calm and control he expected of Yellich, and the excitement he could understand: a body in a shallow grave, with artefacts that indicated burial within a thirty-year time gap was indeed

26

'interesting'. Here was a story, here was a puzzle to be solved.

He continued driving along the pasty grey-coloured road which, with its arrow straightness, said 'Roman' to Hennessey, and then slowed as he saw a group of vehicles parked against the verge ahead of him, police vehicles, a black windowless mortuary van and, to his delight, a red and white Riley, circa 1947, a graceful vehicle of an earlier era, long bonnet, black roof and running boards.

He slowed to a halt beside the Riley and stepped out of his car, reaching for his straw hat as he did so – the sun was high in the sky and beat down. Definitely straw hat weather. He stepped on to the baked-hard verge and strode down the narrow baked-hard path towards the wood where a constable in a white shirt stood and where a blue and white police tape hung across the entrance, a few feet above the path. The constable sheepishly looked to one side and then down at his feet as Hennessey strode towards him and then, when Hennessey was within six feet of him, the constable looked up, held brief eye contact, half saluted and said, 'Afternoon, sir,' and lifted the tape to allow the Chief Inspector easy access to the wood.

Hennessey mumbled a reply to the constable and stepped into the shade of the wood, brushing away a swarm of flies which had congested near the entrance and saw an inflated blue and white forensic tent which stood in the centre of a clearing. A sergeant and two constables stood outside the tent and the sergeant, noticing Hennessey approach, walked to the tent and spoke to someone and then stepped back again. Moments later, as if in response to whatever the sergeant had said, Yellich, head bowed, emerged from the tent and then stood up, smiling at Hennessey. 'Thank you for coming so promptly, sir.'

'I would have been here earlier,' Hennessey pondered the scene, 'but I went out for lunch. You know what I feel about that canteen fodder, that which is laughingly known as food. We have a body, I believe?'

'Yes, sir...' Yellich turned and indicated the forensic tent. Hennessey stepped inside and instantly found it stuffy and difficult to breathe, but the tent was doing its job; preserving the crime scene.

'As you see, sir, we're a bit late to jump into action, to catch the first all important twenty-four hours of a murder investigation.' Yellich followed Hennessey into the tent. 'A bit late by a long way.'

'I'll say.' Hennessey looked down at the skeleton in the shallow grave. 'But it's murder all right.'

'Inspector.' Louise D'Acre kneeling over the body looked up and without expression of emotion acknowledged Hennessey's arrival.

'Dr D'Acre,' Hennessey responded. 'Can you tell us anything at all?'

'Not yet.' Louise D'Acre stood, a slender, elegant woman in her mid-forties, close cropped dark hair, slightly greying, but still largely black, and definitely black from even a modest distance. She was, in Hennessey's eyes, a woman who aged gracefully, allowing herself just a trace of lipstick. 'The skeleton is male, not a large man ... short of stature in life as you may see, only five feet four or five feet but I'll be able to get a more accurate reading once I've got him to York City when I'll be able to measure the long bones.'

'It is an adult, though?'

'Oh, yes. But how do you know it's murder?' She held eye contact with Hennessey, warmly so. 'I haven't determined the cause of death yet.'

'Assumption,' he smiled. 'And an old copper's nose. The shallow grave...' Hennessey brushed an irksome fly away from his face. 'Folks who succumb to natural causes or

29

misadventure are not placed in shallow graves, especially fairly remotely so in private woods.'

D'Acre pursed her lips and raised her eyebrows. 'A fair assumption, though that's wholly your department, not mine. You busy yourself in your box and I'll busy myself in mine. The hair, as you see, has, in places, remained on the skull and appears to have been blond in life, faded a little now, but in terms of its colour, it would have been "louder" than it is now. Whoever he was sustained a fracture to the rear of his head which may or may not be *post mortem*, but if it was *pre mortem*, it would have been powerful enough to cause death. I may not be able to determine the cause of death after this length of time, unless heavy poisoning was involved, such as arsenic or cyanide or strychnine, which would still be detectable. I'll trawl for them as a matter of course, but they're methods of murder that we don't come across these days, too easy to trace, and too difficult to obtain in the first place. A hundred-plus years ago you might have been able to go into a chemist shop and buy arsenic, ostensibly to do away with the moles that kept digging up your lawn, though in reality to do away with your wife, but not these days. These days heavy poisons are most often used in suicide, but you never know, so I'll look for them nonetheless.'

Hennessey pondered the skeleton, folded into a near foetal position. 'How long do you think he's been down there?'

'Your guess is as good as mine.'

Hennessey glanced at her. It wasn't the answer he had expected.

'Seriously,' she read his thoughts. 'It's really a matter of observation and application of common sense. The items buried here – the tobacco tin, the rucksack – I'd say point to a suspicious death and unlawful burial about twenty years ago. The design of the rucksack is of a type that I remember being fashionable twenty years ago, twenty-five years, something of that order.'

'But no medical indications?'

'Not after this length of time. Forensic pathology determines the cause of death – that's our job. The timing is something the police have pushed on to us and foolishly, in my opinion, we've responded. Now the police expect it. But the further you are from the moment of death, the more difficult it is to determine the time, not just by days, but by hours and after this length of time, I won't be drawn at all.'

'Fair enough, doctor. Well, thanks anyway

... I'll leave you to it.' He stepped outside, breathing deeply, after the stifling atmosphere within the tent. He glanced at Yellich. 'Who discovered the body, sergeant?'

Yellich told Hennessey about Michael Jolly and his metal detector.

'Loathsome things.' Hennessey's eye was caught by movement in the shrubs, a squirrel, he thought, or similar.

'Confess I'm not overly fond of them myself, sir.' Yellich followed Hennessey's gaze, his eyes being caught by the same movement. He turned to face Hennessey, 'But he got a contact and dug and here we are, set to earn our crust.'

'Where is he now?'

'Mr Jolly? He's gone home. I verified his address from a creased up letter from the Social Security he was carrying in his jeans. He was keen to give his address, kept asking about a reward.'

'A reward from ourselves?' Hennessey smiled.

'Or the newspapers. He didn't mind which, so long as he gets his reward. But it means that his address is genuine, if nothing else. But I don't think he'll be of use to us, boss, he didn't witness anything, for example.'

'Indeed.'

Louise D'Acre emerged from the forensic tent, looking uncomfortable, warm in latex gloves, and green coveralls, and Hennessey noticed how she too savoured the more breathable air outside the tent, deservedly, so he felt, she having been in the tent for a considerable amount of time. 'I've done all I can here, Inspector. I'll go on to York City now and await the arrival of the skeleton.'

'Yellich?' Hennessey turned to his sergeant.

'All finished too, sir. SOCO have taken all their photographs, black and white and in colour, from every conceivable angle.'

'Right...' D'Acre paused. 'In that case I'll remain and supervise the removal of the skeleton, that would be better. Have to lift it as it is, in the position it's in and slide it on to a stretcher. If you could get a couple of young constables to assist me? Better make sure they have latex gloves, there are more pairs in my bag.'

'Young?' Hennessey raised an eyebrow.

'Well, they'll have to get used to handling dead bodies sooner or later, and frankly, the sooner the better.' Dr D'Acre walked to the edge of the wood and Hennessey watched as she raised an arm in a sensitive, polite, yet somehow authoritative gesture, in response to which two men alighted from the

33

mortuary van, collected a stretcher and a cover for the stretcher from the rear of the van and walked towards the wood.

'Two constables, please, sergeant.' Hennessey turned to Yellich.

'Young, sir?' Yellich smiled.

'Oh, most youthful and fresh faced, sergeant.'

Yellich turned to address the uniformed sergeant. 'Two of your lads, please sergeant, youthful if you please, to assist the pathologist.'

'Very good, sir.' The sergeant turned to his men. 'PC Coates, in the tent to assist the doctor, and Yardly...'

'Sergeant?'

'Go and relieve PC Scholes at the edge of the wood, tell him he's needed in the forensic tent.'

'Very good, sergeant.'

In the tent with two constables to assist her, one at the skull and the other grimacingly at the feet, Louise D'Acre gently prised the bones from the soil which had held them for the last few decades. 'Lift,' she said, 'gently, gently...' and the skeleton was lifted on to the stretcher and covered with a black blanket. The skeleton was then carried reverently out of the tent and laid on the ground whence it was picked up by the two mortuary attendants and carried, equally reverently, out of the wood to the waiting black, windowless van.

Hennessey watched it being carried away. 'I'd like you to dig down further, Yellich.'

'Yes, sir.'

'Go down until you meet consolidated soil, you'll know when that is. It takes millions of years for soil to consolidate. You've dug your garden, I assume?'

'What little we have, sir, but I know what you mean, surface soil and consolidated soil are very different.' He turned and once again addressed the sergeant. 'You have a spade in the area car?'

'Yes, sir.'

'Good. If you'd get one of your boys to dig beneath where the skeleton lay, just a few inches, just to make sure nothing is hidden there. And you can deflate the tent.'

'Very good, sir.'

Hennessey knelt down and rummaged in the rucksack. A few clothes, rotten and looking as though they were inexpensive when new. The zippers at the side pockets of the rucksack were rusted and would not be unzipped. He became aware of Yellich standing beside him holding a large production bag. 'Better do that down at the station, sir.'

'You're right.' Hennessey stood and placed the rucksack in the production bag. 'Curiosity got the better of me. But you're right, a nice controlled, guarded environment in which to examine this and the tobacco tin, and the contents of both. Where is the tin?'

'In a production bag, sir.'

'Can you see any purpose in searching the wood, Yellich?'

'I can't, sir, not after this amount of time, unless we know specifically what we are looking for.'

'That's my view, but it's good to have a second opinion. So, if you'll finish up here...'

George Hennessey drove back to Micklegate Bar Police Station and parked his car in the car park at the rear of the rambling, red-bricked, Victorian building and entered by the rear 'staff only' entrance, carrying the rucksack with him. He paused briefly to check his pigeonhole and seeing only circulars, went directly to the productions room in the basement of the building and obtained a reference number and form from the officer in charge of productions and logged in the rucksack. He then laid the rucksack on the table in the centre of the room and once again tried to force the zips of the side pockets, and all four stubbornly refused to yield. He asked the officer in charge of productions if he had a knife.

'Pair of scissors, sir.' The officer held up a pair of large stainless steel scissors.

'They'll do.' Hennessey used the scissors to cut open the Terylene of the outside pockets. Inside the top left-hand pocket he found, among other items, a National Union of Students identity card bearing the photograph of a blond-haired young man with a warm smile but with a haunted look in his eyes. He was by name Norris Smith, and twenty years previously had been a student, in his final year, at the University of York, the faculty of Law. 'Bingo!' Hennessey held up the card and glanced at the officer in charge of productions. 'Bingo!'

'Bingo,' was the bemused reply.

Margaret South had not been to the wood, to Norris's grave for four days by that Monday. She had come to notice that the interval between each visit was getting a little longer as the weeks went on. She was, she thought, coming to terms with it, it and her guilt ... perhaps, she pondered, perhaps that was the answer: do nothing. If in doubt, do nothing. Let it be. What's done is done, it cannot be undone ... to notify the police now would ruin her life, ruin her husband's career, ruin their children's lives before they'd begun ... her children ... she sat in the armchair, the deep armchair by the stone fireplace in the living-room of her home moving her head slowly from side to side, no, no, no ... she thought over and over again ... no, no ... for my children's sake ... no. Perhaps when they're up, perhaps then ... but now, it would only dig up, literally dig up what is best left buried. It would serve no purpose ... Then suddenly she stopped that train of thought and spoke aloud. 'Silver!' she called and the springer spaniel on the hearth rug sat up looking at her keenly. She sat forward and spoke to the dog, 'That's not the right attitude, is it, dog? It's not the right attitude at all. That's what is known as a "rationalisation", finding inappropriate reasons for not doing or doing something that you don't want to do, or something you do want to do. Isn't it?' And the dog looked at her quizzically, head to one side.

'Norris had a family. He spoke of his brother, they'll be pining in their ignorance. I can imagine how his parents must feel now ... now I've got children of my own. Now I can understand how Norris's parents must have felt once they realised he'd disappeared, and remained missing for twenty years...' She leaned forward and held the spaniel's head gently in both her hands. 'That must be the worst, the not knowing, it's worse than the worst fears being confirmed ... it must be. At least then you know, at least you can grieve ... you can lay a wreath on the grave. But what to do?'

Margaret South massaged the spaniel's ear, 'No ... it's not what to do. I know what to do, what I have to do ... there's no decision to be made, Silver, there isn't. There just isn't, not about what to do. The issue is when – when do I do it? Sooner, so Norris's family can be released from their anguish ... but when my family will be destroyed? Or later ... when my family will be old enough to cope with it, but Giles and I have made a "no secrets pact" and I've already broken it by keeping it from him for this amount of time? I have to tell him ... it's looking like an earlier rather than later call, little brown and white dog. But not yet. I'll have a couple of gins and then blurt it out...

'Giles South, general practitioner, with a semi-rural practice, man of good standing in this parish, father of three teenage children, you have a wife who, twenty-plus years ago, helped bury the body of a murder victim, and she knew what she was doing too, because she saw the murder take place. Oh, yes, she did, right in front of her eyes.'

She stood. 'Walk!' she said and the spaniel barked and ran in excited circles. 'Time to visit Norris's grave, not for the last time ... it'll take me a week or two yet before I'm ready. I'll tell Giles and ask him to come to the police station with me.'

She drove the familiar route from Knaresborough to Stamford Bridge, then out towards Full Sutton she turned the final corner, the last corner of the journey, around which she would get her first glimpse of the wood. As she did her heart missed a beat and she slowed the car to a standstill. Because being carried from the wood was a stretcher on which was a mound covered by a black blanket ... no, it wasn't a blanket, it was a black plastic body bag, the type her husband spoke of from time to time. Her stomach felt hollow. The black windowless van, the police vehicles, the old-fashioned red and white car...

Margaret South collected herself and drove on, slowly. She passed the scene, glancing to her left as she did, so to catch a glimpse of a blue and white inflatable tent just inside the wood, just where Norris's body was buried. It was him, all right, Norris Smith had been found. At least his body had been found. Soon his family will be very needful of each other. Very needful indeed, but at least the waiting, the not knowing, will be over. And the not knowing for her will begin. Could she be linked before she was ready to walk into the police station on her own terms? She drove further on with flat countryside around her and finding a wider than normal stretch of road, halted the car half on and half off the grass verge. She sat staring ahead of her, aware of Silver's puzzlement, as to why she had stopped but not left the car. She was experiencing a flood of emotions, all of which seemed to want to surface at the same time, as if competing for space in her conscious mind but, above all, for some reason she could not understand, the greatest and most welcome of all the emotions she felt was that of relief. For some reason it was relief ... a sense of a weight being lifted from her mind. It was, she thought, a most profound sense of relief.

Two

In which Hennessey shows willing and Yellich meets a comic.

MONDAY AFTERNOON

Hennessey returned to Micklegate Bar Police Station, to his office, sat at his desk and picked up the phone and tapped a four-figure internal number.

'Collator.' The reply was brisk, snappy, efficient.

'DCI Hennessey here.'

'Yes, sir.'

'I'd like a crime number, please.'

'Sir,' Hennessey heard the tapping of a computer keyboard and the collator then said, 'MB, 620 of 6.'

'Six two oh of six,' he repeated. 'As much as that? We're only halfway through the month.'

'Been busy all right, sir, six hundred and twenty reported crimes since the first of the month, but mostly very minor, but reported crime nonetheless.'

'This won't be minor. Open this crime number as a code 4.1.'

'A murder?'

'And put the name of the deceased as one Norris Smith, name to be confirmed.'

'Name to be confirmed.' The collator repeated and again Hennessey heard the tapping of a computer keyboard. 'Are you the interested CID officer, sir?'

'I am.' And again, Hennessey heard the tapping of the computer keyboard as he glanced to his right and at the view outside his window, blue sky above modern buildings of angular construction and sunlight glinting off medieval stonework, the blend of ancient and modern that is the City of York. A small city, but still a city. It has a charter which says so.

'Right, sir.' The collator's voice refocused his mind. 'MB 620 of 6, this year, coded 4.1, believed to be one Norris Smith. That's now an open case to you, sir.'

He replaced the phone with a 'thank you' and took a new file from his filing cabinet and wrote the crime number on the top of the front cover and added the year. He then wrote 'Norris Smith?' on the front of the file. And here, he thought, here the process begins, for if Norris Smith's parents are still alive, if it is he, then they will be elderly now, perhaps frail of health, yet if ID is confirmed, they will have to have some bad news broken to them. But, he thought, the sooner it begins, the sooner it is over. He picked up the phone again and dialled nine for an outside line whilst at the same time thumbing through the telephone directory. At 'U' for 'University', finding a number of entries for various departments, he decided the most appropriate call would be made to General Enquiries. It seemed to be a safe and sensible bet. He dialled the number and his call was answered by a woman with a warm and friendly voice, and a helpful manner. She listened to Hennessey's request and said she'd put him through to University Administration.

'Graff!' snapped a gruff voice and Hennessey instantly received the impression of a 'just so' office tyrant.

'DCI Hennessey, sir. Micklegate Bar Police Station, York.'

'Yes, Mr Hennessey.' His manner was efficient, a man who took his job seriously. So thought Hennessey.

'We're seeking information about a student of the university, specifically a former student.'

'Yes?'

'A young man by the name of Norris Smith. Faculty of Law, according to his student ID card. He was in his third year, twenty-two years ago.'

'Now he'll be forty-three years old ... mid-career.'

'Had he lived, he would.'

'Oh...' Graff paused. 'I see ... what information do you require?'

'His address. Particularly his home address, not the address of his university accommodation of the time.'

'We wouldn't have that anyway, just a record of his home address. I'll have to phone you back. It'll mean going back into the records, so I don't have the information to hand. But I'd have to phone you back anyway.'

'Of course.' Hennessey gave Graff the number of Micklegate Bar Police Station. Graff said he'd come back as soon as he could, definitely before the end of the day. Hennessey replaced the phone coincidentally with a soft, reverential tap on the frame of his office doorway. He turned. 'Yellich,' he smiled, 'come in and take a pew.' He indicated a chair in front of his desk. 'I've

45

just phoned the university.'

'The university, sir?'

'Came up trumps with the rucksack. Had to cut it open, the side pocket contained this.' He handed the student ID card to Yellich, who read it.

'Norris Smith, Faculty of Law,' Yellich mused. 'The blond hair ties in. Dr D'Acre said the skeleton had traces of what appeared to be blond hair attached to the skull. This photograph shows quite a mop of blond hair. Nice-looking lad, sharp features, nice smile. Tragic ... a life cut so short and with a career in Law ahead of him – if it is Norris Smith, the remains of whom we found this forenoon. I presume you've phoned the university for his home address, sir?'

'I have.'

'Anything on mis per about him?'

'Just about to do that when you came.' Hennessey smiled and, for the third time within fifteen minutes, picked up the phone and then dialled an internal number.

'Collator!' Again, the collator's voice snapped briskly, efficiently.

'Hennessey here again.'

'Yes, sir?'

'The provisional name I gave you for the murder victim.'

'Smith, Norris, to be confirmed?'

'Yes, that's it. Can you see what missing persons have on that name, if anything? He would have been reported missing about twenty-two years ago when he'd be in his early twenties.'

'Very good, sir.'

Hennessey replaced the phone gently. 'I feel in my waters that we have the remains of Norris Smith. I feel that his ID will be confirmed very quickly. The identity of his murderer, or murderers will be a different matter. After this length of time, it's going to be difficult. Even if we do identify them to our satisfaction, we have to have enough to convince a jury if we're going to secure a conviction, and I don't need to tell you how difficult that can be, even with a murder which happened yesterday, but a murder of twenty-plus years ago...'

'All we can do is take it as far as we can, boss, see where we get.'

'That's the right attitude.'

There was a lull in the conversation. Hennessey thought Yellich looked troubled. He said so.

'Ever heard of a lawyer going to gaol, sir?'

'The occasional bent solicitor. Why?'

'Case once, wasn't involved, read about it. Eighteen-year-old lad in Belfast, joined the

IRA, planted a bomb, killed two people. Did well at his studies and applied to leave the IRA. They let him go, local lad, doing well, so long as his allegiance remained and didn't waver, they let him go. Twenty years later he was linked to the bomb, breakthrough in forensic science, you see, sir ... The Special Branch gave him the seven o'clock knock, by which time he was married with children and a university teacher in England. Went down for life.'

'Nobody's above the law, Yellich.'

'I'm not suggesting for a moment anybody is, sir.' Yellich held eye contact. 'What I am saying is that if the skeleton is that of Norris Smith, and if his murderer or murderers were also law students, then now they'll be solicitors, barristers, maybe even a junior judge or two.'

'Yes...' Hennessey awaited Yellich's point.

'The point being that they'll know how to cover their tracks. That's going to make our job doubly difficult.'

'It is, isn't it? But let's not imagine obstacles, see where we get to, as you said. What did you find in the wood?'

'Nothing, sir. Went down as far as you suggested, into consolidated soil, nothing was buried beneath the body. We also sifted the spoil, again nothing. The skeleton, the

48

rucksack, and the tin of tobacco. That is it.'

'Enough to go on. So what's to be done?' Hennessey leaned back in his chair and smiled at the younger man sitting in front of his desk.

'Sir?'

'What's to be done? If you were the senior officer involved in the case, what would you do now?'

'Attend the post-mortem.'

'One of us will have to do that anyway. Meantime we await feedback from the university and our collator.' Hennessey tapped the phone.

'Not much we can do, sir.'

'Isn't there?'

'Sir?' Yellich felt puzzled and awkward, as though he had missed an important point.

'Private wood, wasn't it?'

'Yes, sir.'

'So. It'll have an owner. Someone to have a chat with.'

'Of course, sir,' Yellich smiled.

'And a press release. I think I'd like a press release on this one. Press releases can be very fruitful. A ghost returning after twenty-something years, and starts tapping folk on the shoulder – that can rattle a cage or two, someone not totally enthusiastic about being sent down for life could be panicked into confessing. It's happened before.'

'Certainly won't do any harm, sir.'

'And may do a lot of good. So, can you attend to those two items? The press release, then chat to the owner of the wood. I'll represent the police at the post-mortem. I haven't represented the police at a post-mortem for some time. Have to continue to show willing.'

George Hennessey walked the short distance from Micklegate Bar Police Station to the York City Hospital. He was a Londoner by birth and had settled in near York whilst still a young man, and had rapidly learned, as the natives of the city had known and had taught to their children, that by far the best way to cross the city on foot was to 'walk the walls'. Accordingly, he walked from the police station and joined the walls by the steps at Micklegate Bar and, as he did so, he spared a thought for Harry Hotspur, whose head had been impaled on a spike above the Bar and had been left there for three years as a warning to other would-be traitors to the crown.

He walked to Lendal Bridge, passing the railway station to his left which, when built, claimed to be the longest man-made structure in the world. To his right, beyond the unguarded inside edge of the wall was the clearly discernible building of the original railway station, with its small curved platform and serrated roof, now used as a warehouse. Hennessey pondered the other folk on the wall, the school parties, the honeymooners, couples deeply in love, and the group of guide-led tourists and one or two like him, solitary figures in the long, thin crowd, noticeably different because, by and large, allowing for an occasional glance to their left or right, they looked straight ahead as they walked and, by doing so, proclaimed their native status. Not dissimilar, Hennessey pondered, to the residents of Edinburgh who glance at their watch when the one o'clock time signal gun is fired from the castle, the tourists are the ones who look up, startled by the explosion.

He left the walls at Lendal Bridge, where the girls had once stood soliciting the foot passengers, female as well as male, but mostly male, until they had been 'moved on' in the interests of the tourist industry. He didn't rejoin the wall after walking the graceful curve of St Leonard's Place, but crossed into Gilleygate and walked down the narrow street, with its jumble of small shops, the end of which marked the boundary between old and new York, for Gillygate gave to Clarence Street, new buildings, longer, more glass than masonry, and then to Wiggington Road and the entrance to the York City Hospital.

Hennessey walked across the car park of the hospital to the actual entrance of the building, scanning the expanse of motor vehicles as he did so, searching for a red and white Riley, the car he had last seen that morning parked beside a green verge on a grey road in rural North Yorkshire. He located the vehicle and allowed his gaze to rest on it, warmly so. He entered the low rise, slab-sided building and walked to the Department of Pathology. He walked to a door which had the nameplate, 'Louise D'Acre, M.D., F.R.C.Path.' He tapped reverentially on the door. After a pause which was too short to be termed imperious, but long enough to assert authority, Dr D'Acre said, 'Come in.'

Hennessey opened the door and smiled at Dr D'Acre who eyed him coldly and he, taking her cue, averted his gaze and adopted a serious, reverential expression.

'Here for the post-mortem on the remains, I presume? Take a pew.'

'Yes.' Hennessey sat on the upright chair beside Dr D'Acre's desk.

'You know, for some reason I thought

you'd send Sergeant Yellich. I don't know why, no real reason, just an inkling.'

'Perhaps it's because I haven't attended one for some time. Felt I had to show willing, as I said to Yellich before I came here. He's gone to see the owner of the wood. Burying a body in a privately owned wood doesn't link the owner to the corpse in the way burying it in a backyard would do, but we can't leave that stone unturned, even if it is just for form's sake.'

'I can understand that.' D'Acre smiled briefly. 'Loved the use of "wood" and "would" in the same sentence, I can understand how difficult it must be for foreigners to master the language. Easy to grasp the basics, but getting into the nuances takes years, so I'm told, and I can understand why when I hear sentences like that.'

'Yes ... anyway, I thought I'd better keep my hand in.'

'Your hand?' D'Acre raised her eyebrows. 'Rather thought it was my hand that had to be kept "in". It is after all my hand that does the work.'

'Form of expression.' Hennessey smiled as he surveyed the room, small, a little cramped, he thought. The desk had a modest working surface requiring Dr D'Acre to keep everything neat 'shipshape and Bristol fashion' as he understood the expression to be. Photographs hung on the wall showed Louise D'Acre with her children at an earlier age than the present, with her horse, a recent photograph, thought Hennessey, and an earlier black-and-white print of a photograph of a very young girl sitting on the bonnet of the Riley being held steadily by a tall, slender, pipe-smoking man in a shirt, over which braces held up wide, baggy trousers. The room smelt of disinfectant.

'So, made any progress?' D'Acre relaxed back in her chair.

'We believe he was called Norris Smith, early twenties when he disappeared twenty-two years ago. All that comes from a University of York identity card, found in the side pocket of the rucksack. If it is he, of course, but the photograph shows a blond-haired young man.'

'Well, that ties in with the observation at the scene.' Louise D'Acre took a pen and wrote 'Norris Smith?' on the front of a file. 'I can always cross out the question mark,' she explained. 'Bad news for someone if I can cross it out.'

'We thought the same, but we also thought it was better knowing than not knowing.'

'I wouldn't disagree with that ... especially as a parent myself. I fear for my children, but knowing the worst is better than not knowing. It's a form of torture, as repressive regimes have shown many, many times down the centuries.'

'Indeed. We're waiting feedback from mis per and York University.'

'He was at York?' D'Acre stood and reached for a green coverall of lightweight material. 'If you don't mind, I'm going to change, the assistant will let you have a pair of coveralls. You can change in the toilets, everything off except your underwear, and scrub thoroughly, especially after the p.m. but before as well. The drill hasn't changed since you were last here.' She paused. 'You know the dental records will be your best bet,' D'Acre said as Hennessey stood. 'Twenty-two years ... they could still be in existence, otherwise we'll have to rebuild the face which will give us an approximation, but dental records will be an exact match. Or it won't. See you in the laboratory.'

'Well, it tends to work.' The man sat on a stool in front of an inclined desk with pens in ink solution beside the desk on a flat surface. Yellich, sitting in an armchair in the study, mused that he'd never seen a cartoonist at work, yet here he was...

'It does keep people out, but it keeps the wrong people out and lets the wrong people in. What I means is, is that the sign keeps out children who are taught to be obedient and socially responsible adults who would respect the notion of private property, but who wouldn't damage the wood. But it stands as an invitation to badger baiters for example, who reason that they won't be disturbed in a private wood, at least unlikely to be disturbed in a private wood.

'I also strolled in the wood a few years ago and came across a number of stones, fairly large stones, about the size of a loaf of bread, which must have been brought to the wood, they didn't look like they'd been dug up at the location, too clean, too uniform of shape. Anyway, they'd been arranged in a circle about ten feet in diameter and a fire had been built inside the circle, or some-thing burned. Some small item. I didn't notify you chaps, but I thought some weird pagan group, some occultists, maybe they'd also been encouraged by the "private wood" sign. And that is the reason why I haven't kept the sign maintained. I'm happy to let it fade and decay. If I encourage folk to use it, it'll have a healthier feel and protect the wildlife therein.'

'That's a generous attitude, sir.' Yellich

glanced outside the study window, a small paved area, a brick wall about ten feet high, trees beyond, blue sky above.

Horace Skoff took a pen from the jam jar which contained light 'wash', nearer dirty water than ink, and wiped the nib and placed the wooden end between his teeth. 'How did you find me anyway?' He chewed the end of the pen.

'Land Registry.' Yellich glanced round the room, framed awards and clearly, also in frames, prints of Skoff's favourite pieces. The man's doing well, financially so, out of cartooning, so thought Yellich. The house was a squat but large new build bungalow in generous grounds, outside which a shiny blue BMW brooded like a cat about to pounce. He was familiar with the work of 'Skoff' who drew large cartoons for a middlebrow national newspaper, but had never known that he lived in York, on its out-skirts, but in York with the Minster clearly seen from his home. He had also assumed 'Skoff' to be a *nom de plume*, but no, his name really was 'Skoff'.

Short, balding, rotund, corduroy trousers and a blue T-shirt, a man who would not attract a second glance in the street, but was one of Britain's leading cartoonists, and clearly lived very comfortably upon the proceeds of his talent. Very comfortably indeed.

'Ah, ye Land Registry.' Skoff continued to chew the pen. 'I bought the wood, Hermitage Wood by actual name, as you will have discovered at the Land Registry, some years ago. I had a bit of cash, land was cheap, the developers were moving in, ploughing up green field sites, laying concrete over ancient meadows and woodland. I thought I'd preserve a bit of Planet Earth from the dreaded yellow bulldozer. In the event, the building had slowed up and Hermitage Wood wasn't at risk, but I'm pleased I made the purchase, now it never will be at risk. I want to leave something more substantial behind me than a few lines in a newspaper. My family will be well provided for and that has enabled me to leave the wood to the local authority in perpetuity with the provision that it will always be kept as a woodland. They can manage it, husband it, clear old growth to make room for new growth, but it must be retained as a woodland and they have agreed to accept it on those terms. But it's mine until I croak.'

'Generous of you, sir.'

'So, why the interest in the wood?'

'Well, sir.' Yellich shifted in his seat, causing the leather to creak. 'You have a right to know anyway, the sign may well be no deterrent to badger baiters, but it's also no deterrent to guys with metal detectors.'

'Horrible things. Loathsome machines.'

'My feelings, too,' Yellich nodded. 'Always appeal to men, never seen a woman with one.'

'You don't, do you, come to think of it? Men must make natural scavengers, women less so. So, what's happened? A hoard of ancient coinage has been found and unlawfully sold rather than being submitted to inquest?'

'Rather wish that was the case, sir. But in fact a dead body has been found. The body was in a shallow grave along with one or two metal artefacts, the machine reacted to the metal, the guy started to dig ... and, well I'm here.'

Silence.

Skoff seemed to Yellich to be clearly upset by the news. He took the pen out of his mouth and replaced it in the jar full of wash. Skoff in his turn looked at Yellich and saw a man in his thirties with the 'fullness' of expression, a sense of satisfaction which he had noticed family men exude. Those family men that are at least happy with their lot.

'It was found this morning.' Yellich broke the silence. 'It probably dates to about twenty years ago, the burial. But only probably. When did you buy the wood?'

'About fifteen years ago,' Skoff smiled. 'Am I under suspicion?'

'Not at all. A private wood, miles from your home is hardly your back garden, as my boss said, but you are the owner of land in which a murder victim was buried. You are if you'll forgive the phrase "a stone to be turned over". My boss said that as well.'

'Well I bought it from a fellow called Ffyrst.'

'First? Strange name.'

'Double "F" then normal spelling, but "y" not "i", single "s", single "t". His first ... I mean Christian name was also unusual ... what was it? Biblical ... Jacob ... Job ... a name like that ... a name of that ilk ... a wealthy man, a solicitor ... Aaron! That's it.' Skoff beamed, as if pleased with himself. 'Aaron Ffyrst.'

'That name rings bells. A solicitor, you say? Doesn't do criminal work, but I've heard of it in another connection.'

'Ffyrst, Tend and Byrd. You'll have probably seen their office window in St Leonard's, gold lettering on frosted glass.'

'Yes,' Yellich nodded. 'That's where I've seen it.'

'They don't do criminal work, I don't

think. One of my friends is a solicitor, not of the class of Ffyrst, Tend & Byrd, but he does criminal work, a bit of a poor man's lawyer, no money in it, he says. Criminal work, that is, no money by the standards of average lawyers' incomes, but it was he who once told me that Ffyrst, Tend & Byrd only take on civil cases, libel and divorces amongst the "Yorkshire Life" set. There is money for a good lawyer to earn, but not in defending a drunken miner who stabbed another drunken miner. Apparently, the firm is known in the legal community of York as "First, Second and Third". But not to their faces, they take themselves very seriously apparently. But the owner of Hermitage Wood twenty years ago was one Aaron Ffyrst. And a mighty man is he.'

'With large sinewy hands,' Yellich completed the quotation as he rose from his seat, and thanked Horace Skoff for his time.

There was, as always, Hennessey noticed, a reverence in the room which had always seemed fitting, despite the lack of life. In fact, the only living things in the room were himself, Louise D'Acre and the small, serious-minded, mortuary assistant, whom Hennessey believed to be called Filey. The rest of the room had been treated with disinfectant and bleach, liberally so, causing Hennessey's eyes to water, and, hopefully, all living things to be been sanitised out of existence. The fourth human in the room was deceased, and had been for about twenty years, and it was to he, now a pile of bones still loosely knitted together in human form, that the reverence was focused.

The corpse, found in the foetal position, had been straightened and now lay face up on the central of three stainless steel tables in the room and was illuminated strongly by a series of filament bulbs shielded behind opaque perspex sheets which formed the ceiling.

Dr D'Acre stood at the side of the table and adjusted the anglepoise arm which hung from the ceiling directly above the dissecting table, so that the microphone on the end of the arm would be able to 'pick up' her voice. 'The deceased is believed to be one Norris Smith, the identity is still to be confirmed,' she said for the benefit of the microphone. 'The deceased is skeletal. No tissue remaining. It is male, by the closing fissures of the skull the age is approximately twenty years at the time of death...' She paused, scanning the skeleton. 'The skeleton is intact. No bones are missing. The deceased was perfectly formed in life in terms of the bone structure, no abnormalities are noted, proportions of the bones appear normal. The deceased was of short stature.' She reached for an extending metal rule and laid it beside the skeleton. 'The skeleton measures sixty-one inches approximately or one hundred and fifty-eight centimetres ... allowing for shrinkage, as the cartilage between the bones contracting and the soles of the feet decaying, one may allow an extra inch or two point five centimetres to give the height in life of the deceased.'

'So, sixty-three inches,' Hennessey said. 'About five feet two or three inches tall. Not a big bloke.'

'Very short in fact,' D'Acre responded without turning to Hennessey. The mortuary assistant stood on the opposite side of the table and two paces back. The table was Dr D'Acre's territory. He entered only when asked.

'Immediately obvious is a massive depressed fracture of the posterior aspect of the skull which is of a distinct linear pattern, that is, the fracture is of a linear pattern.'

'Thanks,' said Hennessey. 'And you're positive it is a male, just to be sure. I don't want to imply...'

'No, that's all right, Chief Inspector. The skull is rugged, a female skull would be smoother, the supra-orbital ridges are well marked, the palate is larger, and of a distinct "U" shape, the orbits are set lower in the skull than would be the case if it was female. The mandible is larger than would be the case in the female and the coronoid process is prominent. Defining a male, and I'd say a male with a very male face, a very strong male face, more of a rugged caveman face, than a finely boned effeminate man. The pelvis is narrow, that is to say the supra pubic angle is narrower than would be the case if this was a female, and the iliac blades, the "hip bones", are higher and more pronounced than would be the case if it was a female. He's male all right. I'll address the issue of race in a moment, and I'll try to determine age at death more accurately. Now, if I could get back to the issue of the injury.'

'Sorry,' Hennessey said, chastened.

'The injury appears linear, a wound caused by the impact of a long, thin object, which is also heavy and strong. It is slightly inclined, lower to the left posterior, rising to the right posterior. It has caused massive indentation of the skull and would have been delivered with some considerable force.'

'Something like an axe handle?' Hennessey ventured.

'Thinner, I'd say. But if he wasn't dead already, this would have caused instantaneous death. Absolutely instantaneous. His lights would have gone out in an instant. Lucky in a way, tragic that he died so young, but not a bad death.'

'Murder? As I thought?'

'Oh, yes. This was no accident. His skull isn't thin, normal thickness. Someone held a long, thin object with both hands and wielded it with all his or her might, had to, to cause injuries like this. In fact I'd go so far as to say the power of the blow suggests passion. He wasn't a random victim. Somebody, emotionally driven, wanted him dead. I can see a shallow grave as a panic induced consequence of a prank that went horribly wrong, but this injury speaks of murder.' Louise D'Acre wiped her forehead with her forearm. 'I think that this is the death injury. Heavy poisons will still be in the bloodstream, hair and long bones. As I said, I'll trawl for them but this, I think we'll find, is what killed him.' Louise D'Acre pondered the skeleton. 'He was white European.'

'You can tell the ethnic group of a person from the skeleton?'

'Easily. Have to be careful with Asians and Caucasians, they can be confused with each other. Asians, though, tend to be more finely boned. This gentleman, this young gentleman, is small of stature but quite heavily boned, so I can rule out Asian as his race. Racial mixing can produce interesting skeletons but this man is Caucasian, ethnically.' She took a stainless steel spatula and forced it between the teeth and then twisted it. The jaw 'gave' with a loud 'crack'. 'The mouth is a goldmine of information, sex and race and age can often be determined from the teeth alone.'

'Really?'

'Yes, really, and here, front and lower incisors, the smaller lateral incisors, those teeth either side of the central incisors speak for a Caucasian person. A Caucasian female incidentally would have very small lateral incisors. Caucasian males have larger lateral incisors than the Caucasian female, but in both cases, the lateral incisors are smaller than the central incisors. Had he been Mongoloid, he would have had molars all the way round, top and bottom. Now, this will help you...'

'Oh...?'

'He had dental work done.'

'He did?'

'He did. Fillings ... and British dentistry, too, by the look of it. It seems that all is pointing to the deceased as being Norris Smith. The dental records will confirm it, if you can locate them.'

'It is he...?' Hennessey mused. 'In my bones, I know it is Norris Smith.'

George Hennessey walked back to Micklegate Bar Police Station, retracing his steps of earlier that afternoon; Clarence Street, Gillygate, St Leonard's Place, Lendal Bridge, the wall, telling the tourist from the citizen, and as he walked he pondered a number of things.

He pondered that he was fortunate to live in such a beautiful and interesting city, Medieval, Roman, Viking – interesting to the point that he had heard people refusing to live in York because 'it's like living in a museum'. It was not a notion George Hennessey subscribed to. The instant he set foot in York as a young man, relocating from London, a little disorientated by National Service in the Royal Navy, he thrilled to the mysticism of the city, the Roman ruins, the Minster, the shops with their narrow front but deeply protruding floor space, giving an insight into the width of the terrace, the snickelways, the narrow passages forming a footpath system within the street system. Much, he reflected, much had been visited on these few square miles down the centuries during the blazing hot summers, and the bitingly cold winters. Much, much had happened.

He pondered that Yellich had been correct in his observation that the first all important twenty-four hours in any murder investigation are long gone, so far long past that he could not, offhand, recall when he had last enjoyed the luxury of a stroll, a leisurely stroll at that, when still within twenty-four hours of the discovery of the body of a murder victim.

And he pondered that he was indeed in love. He was not just in love, but the burning bush of passion for a good woman flamed in his chest and in his mind, and did so again, for a second time in his life, late in life perhaps, but it did so again. In fact, said passion seemed to stand like bookends at the beginning and at the end of his career as a police officer. It had burned at the beginning of his career, when he was a young officer, new to CID, the awkward feet-finding days as Detective Constable Hennessey. And if the emotion had not been taken from him then the object of it had, cruelly so, and had not been replaced, until recently. Thirty years later. For now another woman, another good woman, had entered his life, just as retirement was beginning to beckon. The second flame did not eclipse the first, rather they burned side by side, happily so, for each good woman knew and approved of the other.

He stepped down from the walls at Micklegate Bar, crossed Micklegate and entered the police station. He walked past the enquiry desk and entered the 'staff only' door. He marked himself 'in' on the in/out board, checked his pigeonhole. A few circulars to be read and initialled and a notice about Tom Scott's retirement party.

George Hennessey knew of DS Scott of a neighbouring division, not well known, but known. 'I was stationed here in the army, George, made a lassie pregnant so that was me...' That 'Tom Scott'.

He would attend the party, the man held Hennessey's respect. There was also the cost-saving circular which came round every month, it stressed; always use second-class post, make all phone calls after two p.m., if possible. Beneath the memo about cost-cutting was notice of a phone message: a Mr Semple at the University Records Office believes he has information for DCI Hennessey. A number was given on which Semple could be contacted.

Clutching the paper on which the phone

69

message had been written, Hennessey walked briskly to his office, sat at his desk and, with one liver-spotted hand, picked up the phone whilst he ran the fingers of the other through his silver hair. He dialled nine for an outside line.

'Semple,' snapped a voice after the second ring.

'DCI Hennessey, Micklegate Bar, returning your call.'

'Yes, sir. Mr Graff, my assistant, brought your request to my attention. I have found the information you require. I'll have to phone you back, the university is very strict on these matters.'

'I understand, well, I'm at my desk now.'

'I'll phone you.' Semple put the phone down, heavily so, Hennessey felt. He stood and walked to the corner of his office, filled the electric kettle from the jug of water kept for the purpose and switched it on. He poured granules of coffee into the mug and added powdered milk. He stirred the mixture into a grainy brown and cream mess and was awaiting the kettle to boil when his phone rang. He allowed it to ring twice and then picked it up. 'Hennessey.'

'Semple.'

'Thank you for phoning.'

'Well, Norris Smith graduated in law with

a pass degree twenty-two years ago this month.'

'Home address.'

'Seaview, Park Crescent, Bridlington.'

'Bridlington,' Hennessey echoed. 'Bridlington. Sounds like a guest house to me.'

'Does, doesn't it? What else can I tell you? Doubt you'll be interested in his coursework marks?'

'I'm not. Who was his GP at the time?'

'Dr Ballinick, university health service. He's no longer with us, I'm afraid.'

'His dentist?'

'No record. Students make their own arrangements in respect of their dental health requirements.'

'I see. But we have his home address, that's a major breakthrough.'

'He's not in any trouble, I hope? I know he's no longer one of ours but we take an interest in our graduates.'

'No,' Hennessey said. 'He's not in any trouble, I can assure you. He's not in any trouble at all.'

He was an imposing man.

Very imposing.

Bear like.

Aged, but still bear like. Sufficiently bear like to make the room in which he and

71

Yellich sat seem small, so Yellich thought. Even when sitting, Yellich observed, he made the room seem small.

Yellich had returned to the centre of York, had parked his car in the car park at the rear of Micklegate Bar Police Station, but rather than enter the building, he walked back and out of the car park and, unknown to him, traced the steps of George Hennessey of earlier that afternoon. Being a man of York, he had grown up knowing the value of walking the walls from an early age and so he too joined the walls at Micklegate Bar, and left it at Lendal Bridge, as indeed he had to. He had once visited Chester and envied its citizens a medieval wall that was still complete. But York's 'walls' have, over time, been reduced to three sections, from Skeldergate Bridge to Lendal Bridge, part of which section he was presently walking. His particular favourite section was from Bootham Bar to Jewbury, with its view overlooking Deans Park, the Minster, and the beautiful buildings of Lord Mayor's walk, and the third section, the dullest in Yellich's view, but still interesting, from Navigation Road to Tower Street.

He walked as Hennessey had done a few hours earlier, across Lendal Bridge glancing at the blue Ouse as he did so and observed

72

the progress of a single scull being rowed against the current by a female oar, lemon haired, rugby shirt, pulling strongly with a slow but powerful rhythm. A student at the university, he thought. He envied her her privilege.

He walked past the library and turned left into St Leonard's Crescent, but here, unlike George Hennessey, his journey ended. For here, somewhere along the graceful curve of this Georgian crescent were the offices of Ffyrst, Tend & Byrd. He walked slowly along the terrace, looking mainly to his left, the right-hand side, the western side being largely but not wholly occupied by the Theatre Royal. He located the offices almost exactly opposite the main entrance of the theatre, a black gloss door, the golden lettering on the frosted glass of each of the windows of the three storeys of the one time 'town house' of a wealthy man and his family. He walked up to the door and pressed a button next to a metal speaker. He heard the doorbell jangle harshly in the hallway and immediately, a soft, female voice was heard in the speaker, 'Hello, Ffyrst, Tend & Byrd.'

'Police,' said Yellich. 'DC Yellich to see Mr Ffyrst.'

'Do you have an appointment?'

'No.'

'Wait a moment, please.' Click. Yellich waited, turning to glance up and down the terrace, he didn't want to stand facing a door. It didn't look correct, he thought, too obsequious, too obsequious by half.

He enjoyed the progress of an open horse-drawn carriage, a maroon-coloured vehicle with black spoked wheels pulled by a large mare with a shiny brown coat, being driven by a man in a Victorian coachman's uniform. The tourist season was in full swing, though as it passed at that moment, the carriage had no passengers. The pavement, though, was crowded with foot passengers, family groups in the main, one or two parties, one or two individuals, the latter, 'Like me', he thought, 'living here with a job to do'.

'Mr Ffyrst asked if it's important?'

Yellich turned. 'It is,' he said into the grill mounted on the wall.

'A moment, please.' Click.

Yellich, once again faced outwards and watched the horsedrawn carriage turn sedately into Museum Street and proceed down towards Lendal Bridge, followed by a patient, single decker Rider York, cream with red lettering. Above, in the blue vastness, above the sharply angled medieval rooftops, a single vapour trail spanned the sky, an airliner flying from continental Europe to North America. Yellich pondered the captain speaking to the passengers, 'We are now flying over England, the city of York will be visible to passengers on the starboard side of the aircraft.'

'Push the door, please.' Click.

Yellich pushed the door and stepped into a cavernous hallway with a brown carpet stretching before him. The walls were painted with a gentle pastel shade of yellow, the columns picked out in white. He shut the door behind him, and with it the noise of St Leonard's Place. Within the building, all was quiet. To his right, a glass panel slid open and a bespectacled secretary of pleasant appearance smiled at him. 'Mr Yellich?'

'Yes.' Yellich showed his ID. 'To see Mr Ffyrst.'

'Take the stairs to the first floor and turn left, please.' The glass panel shut.

Yellich ascended the stair, noticing a large, crystal chandelier hanging from a black chain from the vaulted ceiling some twenty or more feet above him. One could, he thought, get used to gracious living. At the top of the stairs, on the first floor landing, Yellich turned left and saw a large door, painted gloss black, like the front door of the building, and with a brass plate screwed to the door on which the name Aaron Ffyrst was engraved. He approached the door and knocked it with the policeman's knock – tap, tap … tap – soft, measured, authoritative.

'Come,' said instantly upon his knock, without the pause that Yellich had anticipated.

Yellich opened the door and entered a room which seemed vast to him, a huge room at the rear of the building, with a large sash window which he fancied would look out and down upon a walled rear garden. And then he saw the huge frame of Aaron Ffyrst, and from that moment, the room looked small. He stood as Yellich entered, and Yellich fancied that never in his life had he seen, at least been in the presence of a larger man. Six and a half feet tall at least, he thought, short clipped silver hair, a full cheeked face. Probably a thin face in his youth, but the years had allowed the cheeks to bulge, and redden. He wore a grey suit and a blue tie and a silk shirt. He extended a paw as Yellich walked across the carpet to the chair in front of his desk. 'Mr Yellich. How may I help you?'

'A few questions, sir.' Yellich felt his hand

76

to be consumed by Ffyrst's.

'Please, sit down.' Ffyrst indicated the chair in front of his desk. Yellich sat in the upright but leather upholstered chair and looked at Ffyrst's desk. It appeared antique. Then his eyes were drawn to Ffyrst, who fixed him with a gimlet stare, small, piercing eyes, from a large face atop a huge frame. 'Well, sir, I understood that you once owned a parcel of woodland.'

'Specifically?'

'Hermitage Wood, near Stamford Bridge.'

'Yes, I did. I sold it fourteen or fifteen years ago to a cartoonist fella. He wanted to preserve the wildlife, he said. Bless him. But he paid good money for it, paid the asking price. Never thought I'd get the asking price, but he paid it. Sold it to get into housing, the housing market was depressed, you see, had to go up. Bought at the right time, houses shot up in value over the next few years. Sold them, nearly doubled my money in five years. Went back into housing, student lets, The Yorkshire Property Company, has houses in every university town in the county, Hull, York, Leeds, Bradford, Sheffield, Huddersfield. About five hundred properties all told, Ffyrst smiled a broad, self-confident, smug smile, so Yellich thought, an 'I'm all right, Jack', sort of smile. 'But you didn't come here about that, methinks?'

'No, indeed. Tell you the truth, I'm not sure why I'm here.' Ffyrst's eyes narrowed and Yellich saw a man with a short fuse.

'Please explain yourself, Mr Yellich. Time is money. And I don't come cheap.'

'Did you own Hermitage Wood, twenty-one, or -two years ago?'

'Yes. I bought it when my son was ten years old, told him it was his wood. I wanted to install the notion of the importance of property ownership in him at an early age. I let him run about exploring his wood, all five hundred acres of it. Then he and I painted a sign saying "Private Wood – Keep Out" and nailed it to a tree. Nobody took any damn notice of it, but Bernard tasted property ownership. He was ten then, now he's forty-three. So I bought Hermitage Wood thirty-three years ago, sold it fifteen years ago. About.'

'A body has been discovered buried in the wood.'

'A body!'

'A human body. Of the male sex. Because of items found in the grave, we can date the burial to be about twenty years ago, recent enough for us to be interested. Anything over seventy years old, we have no interest in.'

'Even though the perpetrator could still be alive?'

'Yes. We don't prosecute unless there is a purpose to be served. If a perpetrator of a crime, even a murder, seventy years ago was an adult at the time, he'd be eighty-eight years old now. We'd interview him if he was in possession of his faculties, but the CPS wouldn't prosecute.'

'It would serve no purpose. Yes, I can see that ... I don't do criminal work, though, otherwise I would have known that.'

'Of course.'

'Well, I don't see how I can help you, Mr Yellich. There may well have been a sign saying "Private Wood" but it didn't keep folk out, like I said. Can't remember anything happening twenty years ago ... no ruction in the wood, no damage, signs of violence or anything like that ... I see what you mean when you say you don't know why you're here.'

It was Monday, fourteen hours fifty-one.

Wild Man Sean the Suicide Pilot lurked in the snickelway, just out of sight, watching Coppergate. He knew the man would walk down Coppergate. Paul had told him. He'd done a dry run the previous night, and Paul

79

had been right. He'd been right about the time the man walked down Coppergate and he'd been right about the man's dress, blue waterproof, always wears a blue waterproof, 'that's why he's a socialist, can't afford anything else'. Wild Sean rested and waited. To an observer, he looked wild, a mop of ginger hair, a flat nose, gap toothed when he smiled or laughed or snarled. A ruddy face from too much drinking, and only one kidney. He'd lost the other to the booze. He made no secret of it, yet still hit the bottle like it wouldn't hit him back. That's why he was known as the 'suicide pilot'. He knew folk called him the 'suicide pilot', he knew and he didn't care.

He put his hand in his pocket, the deep pocket of his donkey jacket, hot to wear this time of year, but it was evening, getting cold, and he had difficulty keeping the cold out these days, and he curled his fingers round the handle of the cosh. He'd made it himself, a round, wooden handle with a metal hoop at the end, a padlock, then twelve inches of three-eights chain and a second very heavy padlock at the end of the chain. Fractured skull guaranteed, death possible and, on special request, certain. Then he saw the man, a slender, slight figure, walking slowly, head bowed as if in

thought. Wild Man stepped into Coppergate and followed him.

A few people were about, it was close on
eleven p.m., the pubs would soon be shutting, the time to do it was now. He glanced
behind him, no one was following closely.
As soon as the man turned the corner into
Clifford Street he'd close up, and if Clifford
Street was deserted ... He walked fast, but
silently in training shoes and was just six
feet behind the man when he turned into
Clifford Street. Wild Man Sean followed,
the pavement was deserted, no one behind.
He pulled out the cosh and brought it down
on the man's head. He heard it 'crack',
heard the man groan, and he ran away.

He knew a pub which served after hours,
where a man could get a late drink.

It was Monday evening and the Minster
clock struck eleven.

Connie Kerr sat at her window, her bedroom window, light off, behind the lace
curtain. There was not much she didn't see
of what happened in the street. But now it
was one a.m., it had gone quiet, the row of
terraced houses were mostly in darkness. It
was still, save for a scurrying cat. Then he
came round the corner, swaying with too
much drink in him. Wild Man Sean, bad

81

man Sean, the suicide pilot, but not so drunk he didn't stop to check the doors on his white van were locked. Not so drunk. Not so drunk as she had seen him on occasions. It had been the only movement in the street since excitable Johnny Fuller ran up and down the street, notebook in hand, writing down all the car registration numbers to take home and show his mother.

Three

In which a time capsule is opened.

TUESDAY MORNING AND AFTERNOON

Margaret South feigned sleep. She well knew her husband, as any wife would know her husband after twenty years of marriage. She knew him to be a sensitive man, she knew his finely tuned antennae had already picked up that 'something' was bothering her and had asked her what 'it' was. She had replied in a soft but firm voice assuring him that 'nothing' was bothering her, 'It's all well really, it's just that I got irritated today and it'll leave me soon.'

'Do you want to talk about it?'

'No,' she had said. 'It'll evaporate.' And she had smiled and hidden herself behind that day's edition of the *Guardian*. She avoided him that evening by busying herself in the kitchen, cooking meals and freezing them for later consumption, and by cleaning the oven. The oven didn't need cleaning, but it was heaven sent, ideal for hiding her head as tears welled up inside her and she scrubbed the anger and the confusion out of her. And the thought of turning on the gas was not idle, nor fanciful, nor fleeting. She later hid in the bathroom, soaking in a long bath, allowing the tears to flow freely. It had all come so quickly, so suddenly. The memory was bad enough, it took her days to put the episodes in order and even then there were blanks. But she had had no time to decide what to do because no sooner had she started to visit the dreadful place, by which process she hoped to be able to make a decision, than the body was discovered. The thin sliver of hope that the police activity she had witnessed might have been in respect of another incident coincidentally happening in the same wood had been dispelled by the lead story on the six thirty BBC Regional News programme.

A serious-faced *Look North* presenter told viewers of the 'grim discovery of a body, a male body which had been buried in a shallow grave in Hermitage Wood near Stamford Bridge. Police indicate the body may have been buried there for up to twenty-five years'.

It was Norris. Norris's body had been found. Now she felt the pressure on her, and yet mixed with all the emotions was the ever-present and deeply profound sense of relief. Then, with all the tear tracks soaped and scrubbed and wiped away, she slid into bed next to her husband and murmured a sleepy sounding 'Goodnight', but remained awake, her mind racing, staring at the clock on the bedside cabinet, and remained awake and staring at the luminous dial until her husband's regular rhythmic snores filled the bedroom. She then slithered silently out of the bedroom, wound herself into her dressing-gown and crept downstairs in the darkness and sat in the kitchen, fondling Silver's ears, who was clearly delighted with her unexpected presence.

She made herself a mug of instant coffee, then another and another, and when she was awash with the liquid she felt the urge to go outdoors. She switched off the alarm and unlocked the back door, taking Silver with her, stood on the patio at the rear of the house. It was June, the night was warm, the day had been hot and the stone of the patio was pleasantly cool, but not cold, beneath her bare feet. The air was still, smelled of the countryside, vegetation and manure, but healthily so. An owl hooted.

And all this, her husband, her children, the beautiful home could all be taken from her, and probably would be. Just as life had been taken from Norris Smith all those years ago with that savage blow to the back of his skull. Except she would justifiably lose her freedom, but little Norris, with no justification at all lost not just his freedom, but his life, and had lost his life at the age of twenty-one when all was ahead of him. He hadn't been noticed missing except by his family. By the time of the dread day, they had all taken their degrees and had dispersed to lay the foundations of their careers, 'the years of advancement', so called. They had said, they had told each other, 'these days you're going to get as far as you're going to go by the time you're thirty', and those who were career orientated had left knowing that final exams were not the end, but the beginning, and had become focused on their career plans. She had no career aspirations, wanting only marriage and a family, but nonetheless she too was facing her own future.

It was, she thought, as the owl hooted again, and something fast, a bat perhaps, darted overhead from her left to her right, it was as though they all stood in a circle facing inwards for three years, all known to the others, and if Norris had been murdered then, he would have been noticed missing by his fellow undergraduates and by the university. But they had taken their finals, had had the award ceremony, had officially left the university, the individuals of the circle had, it seemed, turned outwards, away from each other, seeing only their future. But the network was still partially in existence, people kept in touch with selected individuals, but the group itself had broken up. It was at that phase that Norris had been murdered, missed by then only by his family because he wasn't a popular student, and frankly, she thought, nobody was inclined to keep in touch with him. It was frighteningly, chillingly easy for such people, the marginalised people, to go missing. He would have been reported missing to the police by his family, but the police didn't question any of his former fellow students, not one of them. No longer integrated at all, the police, she assumed, had no personal contacts of his to interview. All they could do was open a missing person's file, take his name, a recent photograph and wait until he turned up. Now he had turned up, this ... no, now yesterday morning, he had turned up.

Yesterday he was known to the police as a missing person. Soon, later that day, or the day after, he would be known to the police as a murder victim.

Something rustled in the shrubs. A hedgehog, she thought. The owl, the hedgehog, the bats, the day, the night, life was going on, and was going on without her. Her life was closing down, her horizons rushed inwards.

She owed it to Norris, to his family, to walk into a police station.

She owed it to her husband and her children to stay away from the police station.

She went back inside the house, locking the door and resetting the alarm behind her. She went to the study and searched the shelves, running her fingers along the spines of her textbooks, books she had not opened for more than twenty years, but which had served to impress and stimulate her children, giving them somebody to follow. She found Smith and Hogans, Criminal Law, took it from the shelf and sat down at the desk. She consulted the section about 'Assistance to a Criminal' and found the Accessory and Abettors Act of 1861, Section 8, as amended by the Criminal Law Act of 1977, Section 1. She read the wording and it seemed to her to be an Act forbidding the assistance to a criminal 'before or during'. The Criminal Law Act of 1967,

Section 4, on the other hand, had a chilling resonance:

Where a person without lawful authority commits an arrestable offence, any other person who knowingly or believing him to be guilty of the offence, or some other arrestable offence does without lawful authority or reasonable excuse any act with intent to impede his apprehension or prosecution shall be guilty of an offence.

It recommended that the penalty for any person found guilty of contravening said Act were periods of imprisonment of three, five, seven or ten years, depending on the crime committed by the other person. She closed the book silently, with a hollow feeling in the pit of her stomach. So that was it. Since the crime committed by the other person was murder, she was facing ten years in gaol.

Gaol. She had once been in a prison cell. It had been part of her training and orientation when she first became a magistrate: a prison visit. She had gone into the cells and had the experience of the metal door clanging shut, isolating her from the world in a hard, cold, little box. At her age, she valued the years of her life that remained, she viewed freedom as a precious gift not to be taken for granted, she pondered the prospect of certainly the remainder of her fifth decade of life being spent in prison. What would it do to her family? What would it do to her? If only ... if only ... if only ... and could she cope with prison? The woman who'd come before her and the other magistrates and who had been given custodial sentences, large women, very large, embittered women, how would she survive being caged up with them? And they'd turn on her, she was 'posh', and worse, a magistrate.

Margaret South glanced out of the window. Dawn was beginning to rend the black sky. She crept back upstairs, crept back into the bedroom, noticing her husband had stopped snoring. Skilfully, she eased herself into the bed and lay still. Her husband moved, he felt for her body and, finding it, ran his hand slowly, gently and sensitively up and down her thigh. 'Soon,' he said. 'One day soon, you will tell me what's bothering you.'

George Hennessey slept with the curtains open. It was a habit of some twenty years standing. Being light sensitive in his sleep he had found that the practice ensured that he rarely overslept, even in winter. That morning, he rose at seven thirty feeling fully refreshed after a nourishing sleep and during which he had enjoyed a curious dream in which he and a few others had been trapped in a room with a Siberian tiger and had spent an agonising time endeavouring not to antagonise the beast. Hennessey had noticed this often, that his dreams frequently involved the presence of large and ferocious animals, animals of awesome power, threatening humans who had no natural defence against them. In one dream, a large, fast-moving alligator scattered children in a playground, in another an elephant charged him, but in all dreams the threat was never delivered, if only because he woke up in time. A psychologist might, he thought, make some sense of his dreams, but he didn't attempt to analyse them. Rather, he enjoyed them, seeing them as entertainment, and upon waking gave them little thought.

He washed and dressed and went downstairs to find that Oscar had already risen and gone outside, and was criss-crossing the lawn, re-staking his claim to his territory after the creatures of the night had left with the arrival of the dawn. Noticing Hennessey in the kitchen, Oscar barked and bounded in through the dog flap and nudged up to Hennessey, who patted the mongrel and toyed with his ears. Man and dog: two very good friends.

Hennessey made tea and toast. The latter he shared with Oscar, and after ensuring that Oscar's water bowl was full and his food bowl was plentiful with 'nibbles' he, despite his beloved dog's protestations, left the house and drove the short drive from Thirsk Road, Easingwold, to Micklegate Bar Police Station, York, arriving punctually at eight thirty a.m. He signed in and went to Yellich's office to find the younger man making a mug of coffee.

'Morning, boss,' Yellich smiled.

'To you the same, young Yellich. Is that coffee I smell?'

'Certainly is, boss.' Yellich reached for a second mug, a white one, embossed with a blue-coloured scorpion and the dates twenty-third of October to twenty-first of November beneath. 'Milk, no sugar, isn't it?'

'It is.' Hennessey sat on a chair which stood against the wall of Yellich's office. 'Just milk for I. Now how did you get on with the owner of the wood? Found him all right?'

'Yes, boss.' Yellich poured coffee granules into the bottom of the mug. 'Quite a celebrity, you've seen cartoons in the paper by someone called "Skoff"?' And Yellich went on to tell Hennessey of Mr Skoff and then more pertinently of Aaron Ffyrst, Solicitor of Ffyrst, Tend & Byrd. Hennessey listened intently whilst holding the hot mug in both hands, huge palms encasing the pottery.

'How was Mr Ffyrst, in your opinion?'

'Not connected with the murder. Positive of that, boss.' Yellich sat behind his own desk and tore off the page of his day-to-day calendar. That day's legend was, as Lord John Russell had once said, 'a proverb is one man's wit and all men's wisdom'. 'A very proper solicitor of this town, hugely built man. As a copper, I'm used to being larger or as large as most other folk, but this guy dwarfed me. Liked to have his own way. I got the impression that at home and with his colleagues, especially his underlings, that he could be a bit of a "control freak", but he gave no indication of concern that someone had been buried on his property. Didn't seem to trigger any alarm or guilt I mean, and, lawyer-like, he was quick to point out that the "Private Wood" sign couldn't be enforced. Interestingly, Mr Skoff made the point that the sign worked against the owner in that it encouraged the wrong sort of people to enter the wood. You know, responsible people who want a stroll in the wood with their dog or family would observe the sign and keep out, badger baiters saw it as an invitation.'

'Ah...' Hennessey sipped his coffee and glanced out of the window of Yellich's office at the sun glinting off the grey battlements of the wall as a shrill whistle was heard, the sound of which carried over the small city. A 'steamer' at the Railway Museum was being steamed up. 'In fact,' he mused, 'this whole thing was started by the wrong sort of person going into the wood.'

'The guy with the metal detector?' Yellich smiled. 'It was, wasn't it? You know, I bet he saw the private wood sign as an invitation. Mr Ffyrst made no mention of his permission being sought by anyone wanting to detect in the wood.'

'Anyway, how do you fancy a drive to the coast?'

'The coast, boss?'

'The coast. The Yorkshire coast to be exact. Brid.'

'Bridlington...' Yellich gasped. 'I haven't been there since I was a lad. I dare say it's business, and a solemn business at that, but, yes, I could fairly fancy a trip to Brid, weather like this as well. Why?'

'Courtesy of the university, we now have an address in Bridlington for Norris Smith. Sounds like a guesthouse. "Seaview" if you please.' Yellich leaned back in his chair. 'So, bad news to break, information to obtain. Solemn.'

'Very.'

Margaret South sat in her housecoat at the breakfast bar in the kitchen, one hand gently cradling, caressing a mug of coffee, the other hand she used to leaf through the telephone directory. She found 'Ffyrst' in the directory, not a common name, listed in the business section, but it was a firm of solicitors. No Bernard Ffyrst in either the domestic or commercial listings. It was probably as well, she thought, for she wouldn't have approached him anyway. She then searched for Stapylton. Nothing in the domestic section, but then Paul was a very private person. Paul Stapylton would have an unlisted number out of privacy, not aloofness or arrogance. Bernard Ffyrst would be unlisted out of arrogance, but Paul's need for space and privacy had been one of the hallmarks of his personality right from their first year. Paul had attended very few parties, never got drunk and was never 'silly'. A very serious-minded person, very focused, she recalled, a sharp mind, made for the Bar and it had surprised her when she had read a 'splash' about him in the *Yorkshire Post*. He had gone into business, pioneering micro engineering at a small factory in the Technology Park, and was doing well, very well, by the account. 'Normal rules of physics do not apply in micro engineering.' She had read the quote from Paul Stapylton, and 'you can rotate something at phenomenal speed and it won't generate friction' being another quote from the same source. The paper had also printed a photograph of the type of product produced by Stapylton Micro Engineering, a simple ratchet and cogwheel which would be familiar to anyone who lived from the eighteenth century onwards, she had thought. But also in the photograph was an ant, and the ratchet and cog were about one quarter of the size of the ant. Then she understood why Paul Stapylton was also quoted as saying 'micro engineering is the microchip of the twenty-first century'. But the Bar or micro engineering, Paul Stapylton was the sort of man who would succeed at whatever he turned his hand, or his mind to. In the business section of the telephone directory, she found the number of Stapylton's Micro Engineering. She picked up the cordless phone and jabbed the numbers. She asked to speak to Paul Stapylton.

'Just a minute,' said the pleasant but heavily Yorkshire-accented telephonist. The line clicked and music from Verdi's 'La Traviata' played in her ear. On another occasion she might have enjoyed the music but on that occasion it irritated her.

'Can I ask what it's about, please?'

'A personal matter. Tell him it's Margaret South.'

The line clicked, more music, jarringly inappropriate to her mood. Beautiful, uplifting, irritating, annoying, in equal measure.

'Mr Stapylton says he doesn't know anyone of that name.'

'Oh ... of course, tell him it's Margaret Tennyson.'

'Just a minute, please.' Click. More music. Then. 'Putting you through.'

'Margaret?' His voice hadn't changed.

'Paul ... oh Paul ... what are we going to do?' Then she lost control, all the days, all the weeks since the recovery of that dreadful memory, bottling it up, now, at last, she had someone to talk to and she wept, and wept, and wept. 'We have to meet.'

'Yes.'

'Where's Bernard?'

'At the Bar. He's taken silk and is on his way to the bench. Mr Justice Ffyrst, can you believe it?'

'In touch with anyone else?'

'No. Not really in touch with Bernard, just happened to meet a barrister at a party who's in the north eastern circuit, they are few in number and all know each other. He told me about Bernard's meteoric rise. Simon has become a priest.'

'Really?'

'Yes, really. An Anglican priest. The Reverend Simon James, vicar of saint something somewhere. And I only know that because his church was vandalised and he was interviewed on *Look North*. Nearly fell off my seat.'

'He's the only one of us that ever gave Norris the time of day.'

'Yes. As for the others ... scattered on the four winds ... and you, did you practise?'

'No. Wife and mum, and one-time lay magistrate, that was my not unhappy fate. I'm in Knaresborough.'

'Didn't get far either then. You are not too far from Simon. His parish is in Harrogate, as I recollect.'

'We've got to meet. Can't talk on the phone.'

'All right. The Falcon Bearer, where else? twelve thirty today.'

'I'll be there.'

'We knew you'd come. Eventually.' The man seemed to Hennessey to be in his late forties, a sleeveless jersey, short hair, spectacles, grey shirt, and corduroy trousers with sensible shoes. His very appearance said 'schoolteacher', it could, thought Hennessey, have been stamped across his forehead. 'Eventually, but only eventually, we knew you'd come.'

'It may not be your brother's remains,' Hennessey said.

'They will be,' said the man with a finality that convinced George Hennessey that the human remains in question would indeed turn out to be those of Norris Smith.

The three men, Hennessey, Yellich and Nigel Smith sat in a room at the rear of 'Seaview'. The room Hennessey 'read' as 'retired from service', the heavy brown velvet curtains, the leather armchairs, the solid furniture, the paintings in frames hanging from a picture rail which ran round the walls close to the ceiling, the plant in a large pot sitting centrally on the table which in turn sat centrally in the room. It all said 'time capsule', or 'earlier era', and the musty smell told him that the last guest to be accommodated at 'Seaview' had departed many years ago. The window of the room so far as Hennessey could tell from his seated position, looked out on to a rear yard, then a service road, then the rear yards of the backs of the houses in the next street, then the houses themselves, all tall terraced houses, like 'Seaview'. Definitely, thought Hennessey, this was definitely bed and breakfast land for the families of the Yorkshire coalfields and steel-making towns, two weeks at Brid each summer, then back to hard graft.

Hennessey and Yellich had driven to Bridlington, with Yellich at the wheel, at Hennessey's insistence, arriving at about ten a.m. Leaving the car and savouring the sea air, the salty and fish-laden smell of the town, about them the holiday season was fully in swing, family groups, with brightly coloured clothing, sand in the streets, amid white and cream painted buildings, a flat, calm, deep blue sea, a white boat just below the horizon, and above a blue sky, a blue lighter than the sea, with about four-tenths cloud and close at hand the loud cawing of the seagulls. So Hennessey noticed all in the sweep of his eyes before he and Yellich addressed the business of locating 'Seaview' of Park Crescent, Bridlington.

After leaving the car in a car park with a 'Police' notice in the window and after drawing its attention to the car park attendant, Hennessey and Yellich obtained directions from a traffic warden. They were directed to the 'front' of the town, the esplanade that ran between the beach and the seafront shops and amusement arcades. Park Crescent revealed itself to be a crescent in name only, driving a straight line at ninety degrees to the seafront between two parades of shops, neither, so far as Hennessey could tell, was there a park in the immediate vicinity. But 'Seaview' was there, halfway up on the right-hand side for a pedestrian turning into the road from the esplanade.

It was a house like all the other houses in the street, a tall, slender-fronted terraced house, with a short flight of steps leading up from the pavement to the front door. The building consisted of a basement, a ground floor, first floor, second floor and judging by the dormer window, the attic was also used as accommodation. The cream pointed stone gateposts at the front of the house had been bedecked with cockleshells set in a thin film of cement as indeed had the gateposts of many of the properties in

101

Park Crescent.

Hennessey, followed by Yellich, climbed the steps of 'Seaview' and rang the doorbell and heard the bell jingle harshly in the vastness of the building. A slender frontage did not mean a house with a small floor area. As they listened to the bell ring deep within the building, both Hennessey and Yellich realised that the houses on Park Crescent in respect of their floor areas extended a long way back from their front doors. It was a 'deep' terrace, clearly so. Like the terraces of Medieval York.

The door was answered by an overweight woman with grey hair, a puffy, pale-complexioned face and wearing a long dress with stocking feet in carpet slippers. Hennessey thought her to be in her late sixties or early seventies. But she could, he thought, she could well be younger, for there was angst in her eyes, and pain. Hennessey had, like most people, like all people of his age group, known loss in his life, and in his case, had known loss twice, and in both cases it had been sudden, unexpected and cruel. Those holes were still in his life, he knew they always would be, but at least he had known what had happened to his loved ones. The agony of not knowing was something he could not even begin to imagine, especially when the agony lasted not just for days or weeks, but years, in excess of twenty years. He saw then that if the lady who had answered the door was Mrs Smith, then she could be ten years younger than she appeared. Easily so.

'Mrs Smith?' Hennessey asked.

'Yes.' A look of fear flashed across her eyes.

'Police.'

'Yes?'

'May we come in, please. I'm afraid that we may have some bad news for you.'

'Father!' The woman shrieked and turned and ran down a dimly illuminated hallway of wood panelling and faded brown wallpaper. 'It's our Norris ... it's our Norris...'

A silver-haired man appeared in the hallway, clearing ascending steps which led from the basement. The elderly couple seemed to collide, embracing each other as they did so. 'What is it, Mother?' the man pressed. 'What is it?'

But the woman could only point to the threshold of their home, to where Hennessey and Yellich stood, both men feeling very uncomfortable.

The man side-stepped his weeping wife and walked to the door, looking worried, ashen faced. 'Aye?' he asked. 'About our Norris?'

103

'Police.' Hennessey showed his ID. 'If we could come in, please?'

'Aye...' The man turned and beckoned the two officers to follow him. They did so, Yellich shutting the door behind him, surprised at the gentle 'click' made by the heavy door, and comparing it to the front door of his own 'new build' box, allowed himself the thought that 'they don't build 'em like this any more'.

The man led Hennessey and Yellich to the ground floor room at the rear of the house, dim, even dimmer than the hallway, the heavy furniture, the old plant in a large pot, the brown velvet curtains. 'I'll be with you in a minute.' He indicated the old leather armchairs. 'Please ... I'm going to phone my other son ... he's at work, but he'll be able to get away for this.' As he left the room, the old lady shuffled in, sat heavily in an armchair, weeping into a handkerchief. Seeing that nothing was going to be achieved until the couple's 'other son' arrived, Hennessey and Yellich resignedly sat down and waited.

The man entered the room and stood just inside the doorway. 'He's coming. He works in Filey. He's a schoolteacher. It will take him about fifteen minutes to get here. He's got a car, you see. I'll go and finish downstairs.'

'Finish,' the woman gasped. 'Finish.'

'I mean put away, Mother, tidy up. You're right I won't be doing any more today. I'm renovating an old chest of drawers you see,' he said to Hennessey by means of explanation.

'Ah ... I see.' Hennessey smiled and nodded.

'Would you gentlemen care for a cup of tea?'

'Not for me, thank you,' said Hennessey.

'Nor me.' Yellich took his cue from the senior officer.

The man turned and ambled away, descending the stairs to the basement flat, leaving Hennessey, Yellich and his wife in an uncomfortable, stressful silence, a silence broken only by the occasional 'sniff' from Mrs Smith, and the cry of the gulls from outside the house. Too many gulls, he thought, far too many, their numbers have exploded since they stopped becoming predators and found an easier living could be had by scavenging in humankind's detritus. The waiting continued.

The sniffs.

The cawing of the gulls.

An occasional 'creak' as either Yellich or Hennessey shifted their position in the old armchair each occupied.

The man, thought Hennessey, hadn't gone downstairs to 'finish off' or to 'put away' so much as he had realised what tension would be in the room until their 'other son' arrived and had seized the opportunity to escape.

Then, thankfully, a key turned in the front door, it opened and shut, a man's footfall was heard in the corridor, and then a man in his forties entered the room. Both Hennessey and Yellich stood. 'Police?' asked the man.

'DCI Hennessey.'

'DS Yellich.'

'Please, gentlemen, do sit down.' The man sat on the sofa beside, but not close to, the woman. 'I'm Nigel Smith, Norris's brother.'

'Well, we have reason to believe that human remain...' Hennessey faltered as Mr Smith the elder entered the room and sat on the sofa, between his wife and son. 'We have reason to believe that human remains which were found a day or two ago, in a shallow grave near York—'

'Oh...' Nigel gasped. 'The report on the television news.'

'It was carried on the regional news, yes,' Hennessey nodded. 'With the remains was a rucksack.'

'Red. Terylene. Aluminium frame?'

'Yes.'

Nigel Smith put his hand to his head. 'That was mine. Norris asked to borrow it.'

'There was an NUS card in the side pocket belonging to a Norris Smith of the University of York. The university authorities provided us with this address. I take it Norris is still missing?'

'Yes,' Nigel Smith said flatly.

'We knew something had happened,' Mr Smith said. 'Norris just wouldn't go away without telling us. He was always so good about keeping in touch. We have been a close family that way.'

'The identity isn't certain, yet,' said Hennessey.

'I hope it is and I hope it isn't,' Nigel Smith said. 'If you see what I mean. If it is, hope ends as well as the uncertainty.'

'I fully understand.' Hennessey spoke softly. 'We have the student ID card and it would help if you could identify the rucksack. If it has any unique marks that would identify it as yours, for example. But what we really need is to access Norris's dental records. Do you know which dentist he was registered with at the time of his disappearance?'

'Mr Friedmann, here in Bridlington. He didn't register with a dentist in York. Came home for dental treatment.'

'Mr Friedmann,' Yellich wrote on his note-pad.

'Just opposite the railway station.'

'Do you know what happened?' Nigel Smith asked.

'Not yet. But the shallow grave suggests foul play, not misadventure, or natural causes. We can compare the teeth of the remains with the dental records. If they match, the identity is certain.'

'I see.' Nigel Smith sat back. The leather of the sofa creaked.

'It's Norris.' Mrs Smith stood. 'A mother knows.' She stood and left the room. There was the rustling of clothing, the door opened and then closed. Mr Smith stood and also left the house.

'My mother will have gone to the chapel,' Nigel Smith said. 'My father will spend the rest of the day pacing up and down the front.'

'I see,' Hennessey said softly.

'It's how they've handled it down the years.'

'We all find ways to handle it. Whatever "it" is.' Hennessey held eye contact briefly with Nigel Smith, then breaking it he asked. 'Assuming that the remains are those of your brother, do you have any information, or thoughts about the circumstances of his disappearance?'

'If it is my brother, the remains of ... you said yourself that the identity has to be confirmed.'

'Allowing for that fair point,' Hennessey inclined his head. 'But one way or another, your brother has still disappeared, and from a family that kept in close touch, clearly so.'

'Point to you,' Nigel Smith smiled. 'Well, what can I tell you? He had finished university ... it wasn't a happy time for him, he didn't enjoy it.'

'Oh?'

'Well, I got the feeling that he was out of his depth, socially speaking, and I also think intellectually speaking as well. He probably wasn't really up to the course, but he got a degree. But it was the social side of university that I think he found difficult ... well, this is where we grew up, this house – Mother and Father keep a bed and breakfast in Bridlington, parents' bedroom and the living-room is in the basement, Norris's room and my room were upstairs in the attic. The guests occupied the rest of the house, this is the guest sitting-room, or was, but Norris went from this to read law at York and I think he found himself a bit out of his class, his fellow students were very pukka. He had the bits of paper they had, but England still is a class-based society and there is a glass wall which separates one class from the other. He couldn't break through the glass wall. I got the impression that he went with the wrong expectations, hoping for an instant social life, unconditional acceptance and popularity, but he was ill-equipped. He left home cock-a-hoop, and returned at the end of the first term demoralised, wounded, beaten almost. I went to the training college and now teach carpentry. I was in my social class, at my intellectual level, and frankly I don't think Norris was any more intelligent than I am. Norris, though, came up quite hard against the feared and formidable hidden agenda.'

A nice turn of phrase, Hennessey thought, and further thought that Nigel Smith, teacher of carpentry at a school in Filey had probably undersold himself. A little more faith in himself and he could have done better, gone further in life.

'What is a start line for most people was a defeat for your brother?'

'In a nutshell.' A pained look crept into Nigel Smith's eyes, remained there for a second or two and then vanished. Hennessey and Yellich watched as the man's eyes became alert again. 'He had an expression, he would say that he was "waiting for it".'

'Waiting for it?'

'That's what he'd say. He'd also say that he was "having a gentle approach to things". He was difficult to reach at times, very wrapped up in himself, but I think he sensed a massive hole in his personality where self-confidence should have been and that's what he meant by "waiting for it" as though self-confidence was going to pop through the letterbox one morning, and he was "having a gentle approach to things" until self-confidence arrived. He was waiting for someone to pull a switch and he would then become animated and full of get up and go.'

'I begin to see him. Would you say that he was the sort of person that could become an easy victim?'

'Oh, yes,' Nigel Smith nodded. 'Like Danish bacon, he had "victim" written all the way through him. Intellectually speaking, he was probably eaten alive at university, he would have been a natural victim. Probably not so if he had started work in a low-grade civil service job, probably not so if he went to TT college ... but at university he must have become a target.'

'After the completion of the course?'

'That was the summer during which he disappeared. He wasn't doing anything, just

111

hanging around "Seaview" from where you cannot see the sea ... it's a feeble joke. We inherited the name from the previous owner who said he could hardly call a guesthouse "other side of the street view". But Norris just hung around, not looking for a job.'

'Waiting for it?'

'Yes. But by then he was too old to be kicked into action, he was an adult, he was his own man. Then I remember he said he was going away for a few days, to visit mates ... he'd been invited somewhere. Where and by whom I don't know, he didn't tell us, but he asked if he could borrow my rucksack. He packed and left that same day. That's the last we saw of him.'

'I see. I'm sorry.'

'Yes...' Nigel shook his head. 'It leaves a hole in your life.'

I know, Hennessey said to himself. I know, I know, I know. Then he asked. 'The friends in question ... you can't identify them, clearly, but can you assume who they might have been?'

'It could only have been his university "friends". He had no other friends, and mates he had at school he was no longer in contact with. But exactly whom, I don't know.'

'And no idea where he was going?'

'None. But it wasn't abroad, he would have told us if he was going abroad, and the speed at which he left, took a phone call in the forenoon, borrowed my rucksack, packed it with a few items, had lunch, and was gone in the early afternoon. The impression was somewhere local. If he was going further, he would have packed more, and left early the next morning.'

'Good point.' Hennessey smiled. 'At that short notice, a few items, going where he could get to within one afternoon's travelling time. Local, as you say. Do you have any of Norris's possessions to hand?'

'His possessions?' Nigel Smith looked surprised.

'They can tell us a lot about a person.'

'Well, his bedroom is still as he left it. My parents retired from guesthouse keeping some years ago but refused to sell up and buy their small retirement cottage in the Wolds in case Norris should return.'

'That I can understand.'

'So.' Nigel Smith stood. 'I'll show you his room.'

Norris Smith's room, Hennessey and Yellich found, was a time capsule. It was a long, thin space and the room of a young man in a particular period of time, namely two decades earlier. A single bed with a gracefully curved headboard stood against the wall underneath the dormer window; a desk, an upright chair, an ancient computer and word processor, a wardrobe, a poster of York University and another of the city of York, a photograph of a female, young and pretty and thin, in clothing which was fashionable twenty years ago but which to Hennessey and Yellich now looked dated, very dated indeed.

'We haven't touched the room since the day he last left the house.' Nigel Smith spoke softly. 'It's Norris's room, always will be his room.'

It was a poignant moment, but it was also a useful stage in the inquiry, both officers realised that, for here was Norris Smith's life on or about the day he disappeared, on or about the time he was murdered. There may probably, very probably be something in this room with links directly or indirectly, no matter how tenuously, to the murder of its last occupant.

'Who's the girl?' Hennessey nodded to the photograph.

'Norris called her Anna, she was a Polish girl. Her real Christian name was unpronounceable, but not dissimilar to "Anna". He met her the summer before he disappeared when she was over here on holiday.

114

There was never anything between them, but it's an indication of his social isolation that he kept her photograph on his desk for twelve months after he last saw her. I think that they had a beer together on a few occasions, it never went further than that, but he kept her photograph.'

'I see. Do you mind if I look in the drawers?'

'No ... no, please go ahead.' Nigel Smith extended an open palm as a gesture of invitation. 'The wardrobe, too, if you like ... in fact, I'll leave you at it. My mother may be back from the chapel soon, she'll need some company.'

'As you wish,' Hennessey said opening the drawer of the bedside cabinet, always a place he had found to be a promising source of information. He saw a red spiral-bound exercise book on which a sticker advertising a brand of motor oil had been placed. He lifted the exercise book and leafed through the pages and read names written in alphabetical order. 'An address book.' He showed it to Yellich.

'Very useful, boss.'

'I'll say. Few entries, though, but that helps us. It would be more difficult if your brother was universally popular,' Hennessey said to Nigel Smith by means of explanation. 'You see, if your brother was murdered, he's likely to have been murdered by someone he knows, stranger murder is quite rare.'

'Really?'

'Oh yes ... as is stranger rape, stranger theft, stranger crime of any sort is far more rare than acquaintance crime. Which means that one of these names is, statistically speaking, likely to be linked to your brother's disappearance. May we take this with us?'

'Yes, please do.'

Hennessey leafed through the pages. 'Did your brother speak of anyone at university with any degree of fondness? The nearest he had to a mate, for example?'

'Only Simon. Don't know his surname, but he did mention Simon often and with, as you say, fondness.'

'Simon ... Simon.' Hennessey turned the pages of the address book and presently found an entry for 'Simon James'. 'Simon James?' he asked of Nigel Smith.

'Could well be. Lived in North Yorkshire, son of a doctor, if I recall.'

'Ripon?'

'Could be, has to be, doubt if there'll be more than one Simon in the book. It's not such a common name, and that address is in the right part of the country.'

Hennessey continued to turn the pages. The majority of the other entries had Bridlington addresses, clearly friends from Norris Smith's pre-university days.

He turned back to the entry for Simon James, noting it to be under 'S' not 'J' as perhaps a token of affection or emotional need. 'Can you take a note of the address, Yellich? James, household, "The Beeches", Scholars Walk, Ripon.'

Yellich wrote in his pad, repeating the address. 'Sounds posh, boss, sounds like a doctor's address.'

'Well, we'll find out soon enough. But it's a definite lead.'

'It's a lead we offered the police at the time,' Nigel Smith said, allowing a little anger to creep into his voice. 'The time we reported his disappearance, but they didn't seem interested.'

'I appreciate your anger, Mr Smith, but the police just cannot search for missing adults, we haven't the resources. Now he may have been found—'

'Dead ... he hasn't been found.'

'Yes, his body may have been found, now it's a different matter.'

'But too late for Norris.'

'Mr Smith, it was probably already too

late for your brother by the time you reported him missing. Did you attempt to find him?'

'No ... how could we?'

'By phoning Simon James, for one thing.'

'No...' Nigel Smith's voice faltered, 'but there was a reason for that ... what was it? Oh yes, Simon was in the USA. That's right, I remember now, he, like Norris, had completed his degree and had left the UK almost immediately to have an extended holiday in the USA with relatives he had there. In fact he sent Norris a card. I bet it's in the drawer. It was of the Statue of Liberty.'

Hennessey rummaged in the drawer and found a pile of postcards, six in all, and one indeed was of the Statue of Liberty. The message on the reverse said, "Well, made it, as you can see. Just got the return flight to worry about now. Off to Arizona by Greyhound tomorrow. Simon". It was franked New York, five p.m., twenty-fifth of June. 'It arrived a day or two before he disappeared.'

'Placing Simon James well out of the frame for Norris's murder, but he's still going to prove a useful person to talk to.' Hennessey replaced the card in the drawer.

'Simon was about the only friend Norris had at university, took Norris under his

118

wing, I think, protected him. Odd things stick in my mind about Norris and university, you know, how his visits back to Bridlington increased in frequency as the three years of his course went on. He was excited about going, but near the end of the course, he was coming back home nearly on a weekly basis. On occasion, he'd leave the house so late that he was bound to miss the last train, which he did, and would then return on the Monday, missing whatever he had to attend on the Monday morning. Things like that.'

'Not a happy man. It sounds like it was quite an ordeal for him.' Hennessey thought of his own son, who had also read law at university, returning only at the end of each term, referring to university as 'home', spending the long summer vacation with his friends in Greece or southern France. The contrast between Charles Hennessey's experience and Norris Smith's experience of university days was clearly the contrast of black and white.

'Not happy,' Nigel Smith echoed.

Hennessey replaced the book in the drawer and slid it shut. 'On second thoughts, we won't need the address book, there's clearly only one address of interest to us and we have made a note of it. But if you could pursue your policy of not touching anything in the room, it may be that we will have to return and search it with a fine-toothed comb.'

'Of course.' The front door opened and shut heavily. 'Oh, that's Mother, I had better go down.'

'Well we've finished here anyway. You said your brother was registered with a dentist near the railway station?'

Nigel Smith gave the officers directions to Friedmann's dental surgeon of Bridlington.

'Oh, he's a real magpie.' The short, thin, heavily bespectacled woman replied to Hennessey's query with a smile. 'But don't tell him I said that. He'll have kept records from even the previous dentist who had this practice, and he retired thirty years ago. So twenty years back, well that's yesterday for this practice.' She picked up the phone on the counter in front of her and dialled a number. 'Two police officers to see you, Mr Friedmann. They want to access an old record, they say ... very well.' She replaced the phone. 'He'll be out soon, gentlemen, he's filling a tooth. If you'd care to take a seat.'

The waiting room was airy, light, with metal framed upright but comfortable seats round the wall, a print of old Yorkshire, a rubber plant in the corner of the room, a large coffee table was strewn with magazines, mostly women's magazines, though Yellich found and grabbed an old copy of *Motor Sport* and clung on to it desperately. And George Hennessey, finding that his choice was then limited to *The Lady*, *Woman's Own* or *Cosmopolitan*, chose to sit back and quietly try to allow his mind to go blank as a means of relaxation. More difficult, he found, than he thought it would be. One thought vacating only makes way for another. It occurred to him that this was the only time in his life that he'd ever sat in a dentist's waiting room without a sense of anxiety, even though he had never in his life, even when in the navy with its fearsome 'horse doctors', had a bad dental experience. He tried to analyse the reason for the fear. It was, he reasoned, to do with the drill on the tooth, the harshness of the activity which is inside your head, literally, the not seeing, the total dependency ... the lack of control.

A door opened, a very well-dressed middle-aged lady stepped into the waiting room and walked to the reception desk and asked to make another appointment. She was followed into the waiting room by a small, bespectacled man in his mid-fifties, bald headed, white coat. He stood beaming at Hennessey and Yellich. 'Police?' he asked.

'Yes, sir.' Hennessey and Yellich stood.

'To access a record?'

'To remove it actually, sir. If you have it. We'll receipt for it, of course, and return it.'

'Yes. If that person was a patient here we'll likely have it. My wife says I must have been a magpie in a former life. Can I see some ID please?' Hennessey and Yellich showed their warrant cards, but Friedmann contented himself with a glance at Hennessey's only, saying if one was genuine, the other would be as well.

'From York?' Friedmann remarked. 'So, records in respect of whom?'

'Norris Smith.'

'Oh ... the Smiths, they keep a guesthouse, a bed and breakfast ... Park Avenue?'

'Crescent.'

'Of course ... but I know the Smiths, you get to know your regulars. At any one time, a general practitioner will know of his or her most seriously ill patients, a dentist at any one time will know his or her most healthy patients, they being the ones who know the value of dental hygiene. Can't place Norris in my mind's eye, though, it's his parents that I know.'

'You won't have seen Norris for more than twenty years. He disappeared.'

'Oh, I'm so sorry.'

'We believe recently discovered human remains may be his.'

'Oh ... poor Mrs Smith. I have noticed her age – she looks so depressed these years. Couldn't pry and she's a very private lady, so is Mr Smith, a private couple. And Norris's dental records will confirm or otherwise the identity of the human remains?'

'That's the idea.'

'Of course, of course...'

Four

In which two old friends experience a troubled reunion, George Hennessey placates a vexed man and in which Detective Sergeant Yellich is at home to the gentle reader.

TUESDAY AFTERNOON AND EVENING

'He's come into our lives like a revenant.' Margaret South sipped the gin and tonic. She felt she could really do with a double, but she was driving. Odd, she reflected, worrying about a drink-driving charge when there's a much more serious charge to worry about, and which *has* been committed, not may be committed.

'A revenant?'

'It's a word I discovered only the other day and I thought how apt. We were playing Scrabble, a new doctor has just joined my husband's practice and we had a dinner party at our house for her and the other

124

doctors in the practice, a sort of "welcome aboard" do. After the meal we played Scrabble. My modest offering of "ant" was soundly eclipsed by the new doctor who made "revenant" out of it. No one knew the word but a quick consultation of the *Concise Oxford* and there it was; one who returns unexpectedly, especially as if from the dead.'

'Couldn't be more appropriate.' Paul Stapylton raised his eyebrows and sipped his beer. 'As you live, so you learn. Confess I'd rather have found out the meaning of the word in other circumstances, but it does fit, doesn't it? Like a hand in a glove, the poor sod, poor lost, needy little Norris. We gave him a hard time and now he's come back to haunt us.' Stapylton looked around him, the low beams, the framed prints of hunting scenes on the wall, the stone fireplace, a few locally living lunchtime drinkers. 'Never thought you and I would ever raise a glass in each other's company in here again.' He sipped his beer. 'Remember those evenings, the drive out from York in the Green Goddess, just to escape the claustrophobia and the uniformity of the campus? Mix with "real people" we said, a game of darts, and Norris would be the one to remain sober so that he could drive the Green Goddess back to York.'

125

'I still can't believe I forgot it ... that we did it. I never would have thought that it was possible to bury a memory like that, so deeply...'

'Did you forget it, really? Or did you drive it from your mind?'

'Not consciously. But I did succeed in wiping my memory banks clear of the incident. Repressed it is, I dare say, the correct term, but whatever the correct term is, I did it. I'm discovering how my mind works. I'm forty-three years old and I'm still discovering things about myself. It came back in a disjointed way ... I remembered the murder first.'

'Murder...' Stapylton echoed the word with a sigh of despair.

'Then I remember driving to York with you, you gave me a lift in the Green Goddess.'

'We didn't speak at all during the journey. Not one word.'

'We didn't, did we?' Margaret South held brief eye contact with Paul Stapylton and then looked down at her drink, at the polished circular wooden table, the plastic ashtray with John Smith's Beer emblazoned upon it. 'Not even to say "goodbye". I just got out when you dropped me off at York Station. I walked away from you without a backward glance. I wasn't being rude ... I had things to think about.'

'We both did. I just drove away, I didn't search for you in the rear view mirror.'

'It's clear we both wanted to get away quickly because of the association we represented to each other in respect of what we had done.'

Stapylton nodded. 'It was the enormity of it.'

'I think I forgot it within a week. It went as rapidly as that. Then a few months ago, it all came back, out of sequence like I said, but it all came back eventually.' She paused. 'I've been back...'

'Back?'

'To the wood where we buried him.'

'Really?'

'Yes, really. Quite a few times. I used to take Silver, our dog. I wanted to look like any other middle-aged woman walking her dog in the middle of the afternoon, midweek. I thought it would camouflage the motive ... no companion or a dog, that would look suspicious, especially if I was seen on a few occasions, and very especially if I was seen standing on the same spot.'

'You stood on the grave?'

'I don't think so ... I can't recall the exact location, it was dark if you remember, but I found the clearing, it's close enough. I'd stand there, letting the dog explore.'

'Nobody would be suspicious of that.'

'That's what I thought. I went the day before yesterday, saw the police activity, hoped it might be an unconnected incident, but then it was reported on *Look North* and in the *Yorkshire Post*. It's a big wood, but not that big. I doubt if another body has been buried in it, not in the last twenty years anyway.'

'It's Norris all right.'

'Did you forget it?'

'Not once. Not ever. It's haunted me from that day to this. He may be a ... what's that word?'

'Revenant.'

'Well, he may be a revenant to you, but he never left me. He has plagued my conscience all my life since then. I never tried to go back to the wood, never wanted to, tried to distance myself from it.'

They fell silent as a member of the bar staff swished past in a long summer skirt, collecting empty glasses. Margaret South glanced out of the window of the Falcon Bearer, to the car park and to Paul Stapylton's Rolls Royce. 'Well, you've done well for yourself.'

'Yes. Recently though – only in the last

two or three years has it borne fruit, up to then it was a hand to mouth existence for many years but when the fruit did come, well, it was a bumper harvest. There were times when I felt like giving up, but I had faith in the product.'

'Micro technology?'

'That's it, it's the technology of the future, the microchip of the twenty-first century. The future is small. You married, didn't you?'

'Yes,' she smiled. 'Very successfully. A doctor, like I said, three children, teenagers now, in a few years they'll be at university ... I was a magistrate, it was as close to the Law as I got. I resigned when I remembered.'

'Yes, that I can understand. I've got two boys about to start university. I'm in my second marriage.'

'Sorry...'

'My first wife left me. She didn't believe in the product, wanted more money, wanted a better life so she walked out. Divorce was finalised and shortly after that the bumper harvest arrived. She wanted us to get back together but by then I'd met Holly ... she's a lot younger than me, just a few years older than my sons, but we married. The boys haven't taken to her very well, but Holly and I are happy.'

There was another long silence. Eventually, it was broken by Paul Stapylton who said. 'So ... enough small talk, enough beating about the bush, what are we going to do?'

'Yes ... what indeed?' Margaret South looked down at the table top.

'We both know what we should do, both legally and ethically.'

'Yes,' she said with a firm nodding of her head.

'But would it be the sensible thing to do?'

'It's not for myself that I hesitate going to the police, you see that, don't you?' South looked directly at Stapylton. He was now middle-aged, but she could still see the young man. She recalled the long hair and beard, the brown eyes, the chiselled features, the tall frame, 'six foot two', he once told her. But now he looked very, very distinguished in his sports jacket, cavalry twill trousers, silk shirt ... very distinguished indeed. 'But it's my husband, my children ... it'll ruin my husband, he'll have to leave the practice and he's so happy there and my children ... they're old enough to understand what I did, it'll destroy them. If it comes out it'll destroy my family ... my family still needs me anyway ... if I go to gaol—'

'I'm in a similar position.' Paul Stapylton leaned forwards. 'My business, all those years I put in, a broken marriage was a price to pay in itself. But now it's all come together, I lose it all. There's no one to carry it on if I go to prison ... and my boys, they need me as well. If I can keep working, I could create a dynasty that my grandchildren will inherit. I can't lose it all because of something I did twenty years ago.'

'Something we did. You weren't alone, we were both part of it.'

'Nothing we can do will bring Norris back.'

'That's the first thing I thought of.' Margaret South spoke softly. 'The very first thing I said to myself. Whatever I do, it won't bring Norris back. But then I thought of Norris's family, they have a right to know.'

'Now they have his body, they can at least bury him. That's the main thing.'

'They still have a right to know how he died. They have a right to know that.'

'But at what price, and for what purpose?' Stapylton found time to ponder that Margaret South had held her age very well. It wasn't difficult for him to picture this middle-aged woman in a yellow dress, with neat auburn hair, wearing the rugby shirt and jeans she was wearing when he last saw her.

'It's a question of families. Isn't it?' She glanced at him. 'What's right for your family, what's right for mine and what's right for Norris's family. The needs of two families outweigh the needs of one, but the one family whose needs are outweighed does in fact occupy the moral high ground. We have vacated the moral high ground.'

'Our needs come first.' Stapylton spoke firmly. 'Our family's needs. Your children, my children, they're still not adults, not yet. They come first.' He paused. 'You're going to pull one of your ethical dilemmas again. I remember you so well in the ethics seminars. You argued skilfully.'

'Yes...' She smiled, then said, 'I'm so glad I didn't know what was ahead of me, of us.'

'It'll be a classic pyrrhic victory.'

'What will?'

'Doing the right thing. If we walk into a police station, make a clean breast of it, by that means we re-occupy at least a little of the moral high ground, but the cost will the ruin of both our families, the ruin of your husband's career and the collapse of my business. The cost is too great to justify the victory. And we can't forget Bernard. We owe it to him to give him the opportunity of surrendering before he's arrested.'

'We owe him nothing. He's the one that got us into this mess. Right from the start ... even Norris being in the house was his idea. I didn't want him to come, but it was Bernard's house, his party. I knew he'd only invite him to ridicule him, to sneer at him ... to show him what he was missing in terms of lifestyle. "Look at the house my parents have, the house I grew up in and will inherit, compare this to your parents' bed and breakfast thing", that was his attitude. Then he murdered him.'

'What did happen? Exactly?'

'That's right, you weren't there, were you?'

'I heard you scream, I was outside with the Green Goddess, came running in, saw Bernard with the golf club in his hand, you standing up, white as a sheet. Norris on the floor ... I assumed Bernard whacked him with the golf club. Was there a fight or something?'

'No.' Margaret South shook her head. 'No fight, no argument. But you assumed correctly. I've gone over it again and again. What I'm uncertain about is the element of premeditation. You see Norris and I were sitting in the room, the living-room of the house, or the drawing-room as Bernard called it. We were just chatting superficially, you couldn't do anything else with Norris.

What personality he had was so deeply buried that you couldn't access it ... and he had a limited vocabulary.'

'I recall.'

'Bernard walked past, behind him, sneering, a look of such contempt, such disdain. He passed as I asked Norris what he was going to do now he'd graduated. And he came up with that line ... what was it now? "Take things gently," or some such.'

'That was it ... his excuse for not doing anything. Norris-take-life-gently-Smith. I remember now. That bit, that little catchphrase of his, I had forgotten.'

Margaret South fell silent as two men in suits walked past their table and sat talking intently with each other, safely out of earshot. 'Well,' she continued but in a near whisper, 'Bernard walked past again, retracing his steps, but this time he held a golf club. Norris's head was sticking up above the rear of the chair ... the sneer on Bernard's face...'

'A target he couldn't resist?'

'If it was spontaneous, and if he carried the golf club for another reason, to do a little putting on the lawn, for example ... but if he saw Norris's head and then went to get the golf club ... but I saw it all and I think I knew what was going to happen ... I just froze and watched it unfold.'

'That can happen.'

'The contempt on Bernard's face, the might with which he swung the club, and he was a big, strong man, the crack of Norris's skull, a look in his eyes, just a split second but it was there. I think that that was when I screamed. All over in a few seconds. So why consider Bernard? He caused it all. It defeats me why we went along with it, we should have phoned the police there and then. We were law graduates for heaven's sake, if we didn't know the right thing to do, who would?' She fought back the tears. 'We wouldn't have been prosecuted, we could have got on with our lives ... now look at us. We're in a fine mess, both of us have got a long way to fall and we're bringing innocent people down with us, people who were not even alive at the time.'

'We went along with it because Bernard had that sort of personality. He probably still has. He was pushy, manipulative and a "control freak", he had that way about him. He could control people, he could play mind games. I've met people like him since then, now I can handle them, but then I couldn't. I was twenty-one years old, I couldn't resist him, neither could you.'

'Yes,' Margaret South nodded, 'he was like

that. He'd make you do things you didn't want to do, but you did them anyway. How he did it I don't know, his manner, eye contact, his voice ... you found yourself being drawn in. It was as if your personality was being sucked out of your own mind to be replaced by his. So how do you handle it?'

'You remove yourself physically from the person's presence and it's not easy, there's a real gravitational pull to overcome. You have to start walking and force yourself to keep walking. The first two or three steps are the most difficult ... by ten paces you're free of the personality but you can feel their eyes burning into your back, they don't like it when they can't control you. Such people are dangerous.'

'Deadly, I'd say. But I'm pleased you said that. I thought that I was the only one he was controlling, but you too...'

'But we have time. Let's not rush to a decision. The only pressure comes from our own consciousness, and the conscience therein.'

'You think so?' A hopeful look crossed Margaret South's eyes.

'Well, yes, they'll identify the body, but they'll draw a blank after that, none of us can be connected with his murder, unless by the others. If we keep quiet we could even get away with it.'

'But that's it, Paul, I don't want to get away with it. But I also don't see why my husband and children should have to pay for my crime, your family either. We're looking at ten years, you know, out in seven if we're lucky. I looked it up in Smith and Hogan.'

'You've still got your copy?'

'Much dust gathered and many years old, now outdated, but I reckon we'll be charged under the Accessory and Abetters Act of 1861, as amended by the Criminal Law Act of 1977; has a tariff of three, five, seven or ten years, depending on the nature of the crime being aided and abetted. The crime in this case being murder, we'll go down for ten years.'

'Well, speaking as one non-practising law graduate to another, I would have thought they'd charge us with simple conspiracy to pervert the course of justice. Similar tariffs, though, also depending on the initial offence. It all adds up to a lot of porridge.' Paul Stapylton paused. 'Do you think you could survive prison?'

'No.' Margaret South forced a smile. 'I've visited prisons. I couldn't survive ... those bells, those clanging metal doors, the screaming in the night, the fights ... those women ... really heavy women. I'm too old to be taken for their lover but I represent privilege in their eyes ... all those pans of boiling water and scalding soup that'll come flying my way. No ... I won't have an easy time of it. I'm under no illusion about what prison will mean for me. And you? Do you think you'll survive?'

'Not easily. Frankly, the thought of my company falling apart while I'm sewing mail bags will drive me to suicidal despair.'

The conversation fell into a lull, a silence between them in which Margaret South felt a bond with Paul Stapylton, but doubted somehow that it was fully reciprocated, if at all. She sensed, intuitively, something shrewd, something calculating about Paul Stapylton. He was no longer the quiet student she remembered, he had been hardened by the world of business and by divorce. He'd become a survivor. She felt she was with him, but she also felt she was without him. And more without him than with him. She sensed that this man was not fully the kindred spirit she had hoped he would be, and that, more, he would try to take her down a path she would be reluctant to travel.

'Shall I tell you something that may surprise you?' Margaret South broke the silence. 'I feel a sense of relief.'

'Relief?'

'Yes, strange as it may seem, I felt relieved when the body was found. I glimpsed the need that serial killers have to be caught, I understand now why they leave clues behind them because they want to be caught. These last few months have been a real education.'

'Shall I tell you something strange in return? You know what I want to do...?'

'Visit the grave. The grave site as it now is,' she smiled. 'And go there now?'

'Yes ... how...?'

'Intuition. Women are good at it. Would you like to go now?' She reached for her handbag.

'Yes. Yes, I think I would.'

'We'll take my car. Yours will be safe here.'

Louise D'Acre handed the dental records back to Hennessey. He smiled at her, she 'froze' him with a stare and turned her head away. He mumbled 'sorry'.

'It's a definite match,' she said, studying the calendar on her wall. An interesting calendar Hennessey thought, having earlier that year glanced at it. It showed photographs of York, old sepia prints of street scenes at the top of the page, then the days of that month, then beneath the days of that month, a second photograph taken very recently but from the same location as the first, so that June showed Goodramgate 'in about 1919' and Goodramgate as Hennessey would see it should he choose to visit the street that afternoon. The calendar was also sold in aid of a children's charity. He liked Dr D'Acre for that. 'If those are the dental records of Norris Smith, which they are, for no other name is on them, then the corpse discovered in Hermitage two days ago is that of Norris Smith, his earthly remains at least. All the fillings match, all the unfilled teeth match, the occlusions match, and the one missing tooth, an upper left molar, also matches. It's as good as a fingerprint.'

'I'll inform the parents.' Hennessey put the records back in his briefcase. 'They'll want to bury him.'

'I can release him now. The results of the test for poisoning haven't come back from the lab yet, but the tests have been done. I have no further need for the body. But the cause of death will be the blow to the back of the head. The poison test will be negative. I know, my waters tell me.'

'Poisoning and massive head injuries don't go together. Not in my experience anyway.

140

So thank you.' Hennessey left Dr D'Acre's office and walked slowly but purposefully out of the York District Hospital. He had a parcel to post to Mr Friedmann, BDS of Bridlington. But more, he had a phone call to make. Not to the Smiths directly, but to the police in Bridlington, requesting that a constable call the family and break the news of confirmation of the identity of the corpse in a personal way, one human being to another. A phone call would, he felt, not be at all appropriate.

'What happened to the Green Goddess – she did us good service in those years? Doubt if we could have got by without her.' Margaret South sat against an oak tree at the edge of the clearing, poking the moss with a twig. Paul Stapylton stood a few feet in front of her, standing motionless, silent. She asked the question only to break the silence, but his answer was to grow to intrigue for the next day or two.

'Funny you should ask that.' He turned and walked towards her as if grateful that the silence had been broken, but sensitive to the delicate nature of their location he knelt and spoke softly. 'It's odd, but she was never right after that night, that last little load she carried. She felt differently, rode differently, not as responsive, as if something had been taken from her.'

'Her soul.' Margaret South continued to poke the ground with the twig, birds sang, insects buzzed. 'She had a soul. I think you knew that, that's why you called her what you did. Often I looked at her parked against the kerb, or in amongst other lifeless vehicles and I thought, "you're alive you are ... you see, and you hear and you think, you do, don't you, dear Green Goddess" ... stupid, but that's what I thought.'

'Did you really?' Paul Stapylton smiled, his eyes flashed warmly, Margaret South saw that as she glanced at him briefly.

'Yes, that's what I thought. Never said anything, but that's what I thought.'

'Well, eventually I took her to a Land Rover specialist. He checked her over and didn't take long to find a massive crack in the chassis. It couldn't be patched up. I wouldn't have wanted to patch it up anyway, I wouldn't have fully trusted her after that. Sold her for spares, the engine was as sound as a pound and the rest of the kit was in good order, always a market for Land Rover spares. I mean, if you've a mind, you can build an entire Land Rover from the chassis up out of spare parts. I still have an inkling to do it, just for the heck of it, but that's where she went. The dealer gave me a fair price, then he stripped her of everything worth salvaging and cut up the chassis as part of our agreement, rather than sell it on as a make do and mend patch up job to some unsuspecting guy. And I told the DVLC in Swansea that the vehicle was no more.'

Margaret South smiled at him. He was, she thought, a good man, deep inside.

'The crack must have been developing for a while, it was there when we put the body in the back...'

'Norris,' Margaret South said quietly, 'when we put Norris, at least say Norris's body, in the back.'

'You're right. But it was there before that night, but she was fifteen years old by then. I'd bought her from a farmer and he had bought her as an ex-army vehicle, so she had had a hard life before I bought her. We might have piled into her to drive out to the Falcon Bearer for a night on the pop, but for the Goddess that must have been like a stroll in the park compared to some of the things she had to do for the army and then the farmer. Anyway, that night we bounced over the field to get to the wood, in and out of a ditch, needed the four wheel drive for that, with Norris in the back.'

'Thank you.'

'Then bounced back across the field and on the way back we hit the ditch between the field and the road with a mighty thump. I think that that finally did for the chassis.'

'I remember now, I hit my head on the windscreen. I had forgotten that 'til now.' She paused. 'It makes me wonder what else is left to emerge, what other little details will float to the surface? Dare say I'll have plenty of time to think of them, or wait for them to come in their own time. Prison is a lonely place, all the human contact you want, but prisoners are lonely people.' As she spoke, Margaret South looked down at the floor of the clearing and, because she was looking down, did not see Paul Stapylton's expression harden, his eyes narrow, in response to what she had said. There followed another pause, silence, save for birdsong, insects buzzing, a car being driven slowly along the road a few hundred yards distant.

'Something left us that night.' Margaret South spoke softly. 'It left her, the Goddess, it left you and it left me. It wasn't that we were tainted by the fact that we had committed an awful crime, it was more than that, it was the loss of something, and you know what that something is, or was?'

'Tell me.'

'Naivety. We were naive when we arrived at Bernard's house, three weeks in the country, his parents' huge house, sitting it while they were on holiday, a three-week coming down party after the pressure of finals ... at the beginning of it we were naive. And at the end, we had been party to a murder, the murder of someone who trusted us, that makes it worse, and then at the end, we were not naive. And you know, I don't think Bernard was bothered, I don't think he was bothered at all.' Margaret South shuddered. 'His contempt for Norris ... I couldn't believe it when he told us Norris was joining us for a couple of days ... I couldn't understand it. Why should Bernard have invited Norris? The things he said about him, the things he said *to* him. I thought he might have had a crisis of conscience, wanted to make amends for making Norris's life such a misery. But as soon as Norris arrived, the ridiculing began ... I realised then that Norris was there as a game in the party.'

'He didn't have to accept the invitation. He didn't have to stay.'

'You see, I think...' Margaret South paused, as if in thought. 'You know, I envy you saying that, because I think it means you still have some sliver of naivety about you, despite you and I doing what we did in this

145

wood, despite your becoming a hard-nosed, divorced businessman, and becoming a parent along the way. I think there is still some sunray of naivety about you, because you see Norris *did* have to accept the invitation, and he *did* have to stay, because it was a desperate need for acceptance, a hope that this time, it will be all right because it was conditioning, conditioned into accepting what is wrong, conditioned into accepting that you are the pariah, because, because, because ... it's why wives remain with violent husbands, it's why husbands remain with impossible women, violent women even, it's why children remain loyal to abusive parents, it's why the inmates of the concentration camps put soap in their shoes, it made the shoes more uncomfortable and they did that to please the Nazi guards. It's because of that that Norris had to accept the invitation, and why he stayed when he found out that Bernard's attitude hadn't changed. It's what conditioning does to a person.'

Paul Stapylton stood slowly and turned and walked to the other side of the clearing, leaned against a tree and then slowly sat down, so that he and she sat there, at opposite sides, but still within earshot of each other, comfortably so, not having to raise their voices to make them carry to the other. There followed another very long silence, during which time Margaret South could only look at the hole in the ground, dug earlier that week by a man with a metal detector, then excavated by the police, still a gaping darkness, still a crime scene, the blue and white tape at the entrance to the wood said so. But clearly not so much of a crime scent to warrant a police officer to stand watch over it.

'Well you're not naive,' Paul Stapylton said. 'I can see it all now, the conditioning, that's what we did to Norris.'

'It makes our part in the murder deeper.'

'How so?'

'Because we provided the audience for Bernard's ridiculing of Norris.'

'We did, didn't we?' Paul Stapylton nodded in agreement.

'If Bernard was sitting the house by himself, he wouldn't have invited Norris to join him for a few days. In the eyes of the law, we're in the position we were in when Norris's body was discovered. That won't change, but ethically we are fully implicated in his murder.' Margaret South stood and forced a smile at Paul Stapylton. 'It's getting late.'

★ ★ ★

'George.' Commander Sharkey's voice was quiet yet authoritative.

'Yes, sir.' George Hennessey stopped as he passed the open door of Commander Sharkey's office.

'A word please.'

Hennessey entered Sharkey's office, closing the door behind him. 'Sir?'

'Take a pew, George.' Sharkey indicated the vacant chair in front of his desk. 'Are things all right, George?' he asked as Hennessey sat, alert-looking, in the chair. 'Everything's all right? Nothing to worry about?'

'Worry, sir?'

'You know my fear.' Sharkey was a man who, for a police officer, was short in stature. He was always neatly dressed, three-piece suit with a police service tie, black with small white candles burning at both ends, a pencil line moustache, neatly cut short hair. Behind him were two framed photographs, one showing a younger Sharkey as an officer in the Royal Hong Kong Police and the other showing an even younger Sharkey as a Lieutenant in the British Army. He was about fifteen years Hennessey's junior. 'The morale of the station.'

'As you'd expect, sir.' Hennessey cast a

glance over Sharkey's desk, neat, precise, everything in its place. The commander was not a man George Hennessey would like to have to share a house with, and he did not envy the commander's wife and children, their home life, which he thought must be akin to walking on broken glass. 'Over-worked, underpaid, but the morale is high, and nothing to worry about in respect of corruption. We can never be sure of course – we only ever find out about bent coppers when they're exposed but on the level of what you told me about Hong Kong, then nothing to worry about.'

'It would destroy me if that happened in this nick, or any nick in the UK. You know, I would be told by a sergeant to leave the station and spend the evening at the golf club and next morning, there'd be a wad of notes in my desk drawer, equivalent to a month's salary sometimes. And I took it.'

'I wouldn't be too hard on yourself, sir. That was the culture of the place. If you had tried to expose it, your body would be found floating in the harbour.'

'I dare say. I wasn't there very long, unlike some who made a career out of the RHKP, but that money is still in my life, it's in the bricks and mortar of my house. Not a lot, but it's there.'

'Can you blame yourself, sir? It strikes me that it was akin to going abroad and bringing a tropical illness back with you.'

Sharkey smiled at him. 'So what's happening?'

'Big case is the Norris Smith murder.'

'Yes, I read your memo to me. Any leads?'

'None, nothing firm at least. The time gap between the murder and the present is so great that I hold out little chance of an early arrest, if at all. I think it will fizzle out, sadly. If the perpetrator is sensible enough to keep his head down and his mouth shut and wait for a nice, fresh murder to divert out limited resources...'

'I see ... but you'll take it as far as you can?'

'Of course, sir.' Hennessey stood.

'On the matter of corruption ... if there's a whiff ... the slightest whiff, I want to know about it.'

'Sir.'

Yellich drove home to his neatly tended three-bedroom, new-built house, with a small, neatly tended garden, and parked his car by the kerb. As he walked from his car towards his house, the front door of the house was flung open and a beaming Jeremy ran to meet him, flinging himself at Yellich with such force that Yellich was momentarily winded by the impact and nearly lost his balance. Jeremy kissed his daddy lovingly on the face and Yellich allowed himself to be taken by the hand and led into his house. Sara, in the kitchen, flung a powdery arm around her husband's neck.

'How's...' Yellich surrendered himself to a kiss, 'he been?'

'A good day at school and a pleasant hour before you returned, oh handsome beast.' Sara returned to the baking. 'One of his better days.'

'Good.' Yellich hugged his son. 'Pleased to hear that you've been behaving yourself, Jeremy.'

Jeremy Yellich beamed with satisfaction and pride and he put both arms round his father and squeezed him.

Later, after supper, Yellich spent some quality time with his son, and using a battery powered clock taken down from the wall, he allowed his son to show him how he could tell the time, even moving the hands to hard times like 'twenty-five to three' and 'twenty past eight'. Later still, with the clock back on the wall, having been reset to the correct time by Jeremy consulting his father's watch, father and son looked at the alphabet together and there was not one letter that Jeremy could not point to. With love and support and nurturing, Jeremy could be capable of semi-independent living by the time he was in his early twenties, by which time he should have achieved a mental age of twelve years, so Yellich and Sara had been told. Yellich would readily admit to the profound sense of disappointment he felt when he found out that his son wasn't going to be an intellectual high-flier. But as Jeremy had grown, and as Yellich and Sara had met other couples with children who also had 'learning difficulties', then a whole hitherto hidden world opened up and he grew to feel a sense of privilege. He also knew the endless warmth, and love, and honesty and sincerity that children with learning difficulties are capable of, more so, much more so than 'normal' children.

Even later still, with Jeremy asleep, Yellich and Sara enjoyed quality time of their own, sitting side by side on the sofa with lights dimmed, soft music and a glass of wine each. He told her about his day.

'A trip to the coast, and you call it work!' Sara Yellich went on to tell him about her day, the house, *and* Jeremy. 'That, dear husband, *that* is work.'

George Hennessey returned home too, driving the short drive from York to Easingwold and his detached house on the Thirsk Road. He parked his car in the drive and smiled involuntarily at the excited barking of Oscar, who, recognising the sound, ran excitedly out of the rear door, courtesy of the dog flap, and jumped up at the gate which stood between the drive and the back garden, a barrier from the side of the house to the garage. Hennessey entered the house and Oscar returned indoors and met him in the hall, tail wagging, barking, jumping up, turning in tight circles. Oscar, bought from the RSPCA pet rescue, had given him so much, something for him to look after, something, some living thing, for him to return home to. Then they played their game – a bone taken from the fridge on to the lawn. Oscar had to pull it from Hennessey's grip. Hennessey made Oscar struggle for five minutes, releasing one hand, then the other. Then it was Oscar's bone. He took it to the orchard, having 'won' it, it was his to eat and enjoy eating.

The ritual game of the bone over, Hennessey went upstairs and changed into casual clothes and then returned downstairs and made a mug of tea which he carried outside to drink while sitting in the wooden chair on the patio, enjoying the early evening.

He surveyed the garden. It was of course her garden, Jennifer's, the garden she had planned one evening when she was heavily pregnant with Charles. When they bought the house as a young couple, the rear garden was a flat, unimaginative green sward, 'a bit of a football pitch' had said the estate agent, 'but you can do something with it'. And so Jennifer had planned their garden, pencil and paper in hand, sitting at the breakfast bar. She had decided that the lawn must first be divided widthways by a privet hedge in which a gate would be set, garden sheds would be beyond the privet hedge and the part of the garden which lay also beyond the hedge would be turned into an orchard. The final part of the garden, the area furthest from the house, about fifteen feet wide, would be left in its natural state, allowing what plants that wanted to colonise it to indeed colonise it, and in that 'going forth', as she had called it, having read Francis Bacon's essay 'Of Gardens', a pond would be dug and amphibians encouraged. And the plan submitted to George Hennessey was agreed upon. Jennifer Hennessey was shortly after to do one other significant thing in her life, and that was to give birth to a healthy boy child after a blessedly un-complicated delivery.

Then she had died, aged twenty-three years.

It had, he often recalled, been a hot day in the summer of that year. She had left Charles, then aged three months old, with his father and had gone into Easingwold to buy a few provisions, she was walking in the main road, on the pavement, when it appeared to onlookers that she had fainted. People rushed to her assistance but no pulse could be found. An ambulance was called but she was pronounced dead on arrival at hospital. Code 7 in Accident and Emergency speak. At the inquest, her death was recorded as being caused by Sudden Death Syndrome. It was, Hennessey thought, not dissimilar to people complaining of 'the ague' before malaria was identified. So Sudden Death Syndrome has to be recorded as a cause of death until the medical profession can explain why life, for some reason, just leaves normal, fit, healthy, and often young people, often as they are doing nothing more than walking along a pavement, thinking about the next thing to do, and an instant later are lying lifeless, probably dead before they hit the ground. Hennessey's mind had, in the intervening years, often turned on the question of what it had been like for her? Whether it had been a sudden blackness or a transition into the hereafter, or whether there had been some momentary split second inkling that not all was well, or even an actual, equally split second realisation that she was dying?

He had kept her with him in his mind, carrying on for her, as he knew she would have carried on without him because she had been nothing else if not determined. She would pick herself up and carry on ... 'carry on, carry on regardless' had been a catchphrase of hers. And so he had carried on regardless, and had built the garden to her plan, exactly as she had designed it and he felt her to be in the garden, for it was in her garden that he had scattered her ashes. And it was in the garden, sometimes on the lawn, sometimes in the orchard, that each day he would stand and, talking softly, tell her of their son's progress, of his day, his successes, his setbacks.

In winter and in summer, he would stand in the garden and provide Jennifer with a daily bulletin of his life's progress, never missing a day unless on holiday or similar, in much the same way that some folk keep a journal, making an entry each day. Then, lately, just the summer previous, he had with some trepidation, walked into the garden and he had told Jennifer that he had 'found someone' and he told her about the new lady in his life, that they were right for each other, they often work together but she will brook no social or personal interaction during working hours, but he emphasised that his love for Jennifer had not at all diminished, it had, if anything, grown stronger as the years had gone by, and on that evening he had felt a warmth close in about him which could not be explained by the warm wind or the high sun. It was a warmth which came from some other source, but it was there, clearly discernible. He felt that it was like being wrapped in a blanket.

Hennessey walked back into the house and prepared a simple but wholesome meal, lamb chops, and vegetables, then allowed the meal to settle whilst reading an account of the Battle of Inkerman written by an ill-educated, but clearly highly intelligent private soldier whose eye for detail and economy of style Hennessey found breathtaking. Later he took Oscar for his walk; being a brown dog, he, like black dogs, suffered in the heat and so in the summer, a walk after sundown was the rule. And later still, he strolled into Easingwold for a pint of stout at the Dove Inn. Just one before 'last orders' were called.

Paul Stapylton drove home. He was a worried man and he drove his Rolls Royce aggressively. He drove up the gravel drive of his house, a modern bespoke building, built on a green field site at the edge of a village close to Wetherby. He stamped on the brakes and the car shuddered crunchingly to a halt outside his front door. The door was opened to him by his wife. He forced his way past her and into the house and went upstairs to their bedroom and sat on the bed. Head in hands.

'Darling...?' His wife had followed him upstairs.

'It's nothing.'

'It doesn't seem like nothing. Besides, I know you, Paul, whenever you say "it's nothing" it's invariably something, and something big.'

'It's something at work ... a problem with a new project, we have to go back to the drawing board, weeks of work ... all out of the window.'

'I'm so sorry, darling.'

'We'll get through.' He forced a smile.

'Are you forgetting that we're going out this evening?'

He paled.

'The Eddisons.'

'Oh...' Stapylton groaned. 'I can't face them. Not this evening.'

'I could have a migraine.'

'I'd appreciate it. It's not as though we're the only guests.'

'I'll phone them.' Carolyne Stapylton turned lightly on her heels and went downstairs.

Paul Stapylton changed out of his office wear and climbed into a pair of jeans and a T-shirt. He went to his study on the ground floor, passing his wife who sat on the leather settee engrossed in *Elle*. 'They say they hope I recover soon,' she said as he passed, but without looking up from the magazine. In his study, Stapylton shut the door behind him and picked up the phone. He searched his mind for the name ... what, he thought, what was it? Windels ... Windles ... Wynds ... that was it, Wynds. He snatched the phone and dialled 192.

'Directory enquiries, Brenda speaking, how may I help you?' The voice sounded tired, insincere. 'Brenda speaking, wishing I was anywhere but here', he thought, might have been a more appropriate response. Whoever Brenda was, she was clearly at the end of a bad day.

'I'd like a residential number ... name of Ffyrst.' He spelled it for her.

'The address?'

'A house called "Wynds", with a "y".'

'W.Y.N.D.S.?'

'That's it, near Stamford Bridge.' A pause.

'Thank you,' said Brenda, and disconnected her line, allowing an automated voice to dictate the sought for number.

Stapylton dialled the number. It was answered authoritatively by a man who said 'Ffyrst'.

'Sir...' Paul Stapylton said, finding himself sitting forwards as he spoke. 'My name is Stapylton, we met once about twenty years ago. I was at university with Bernard.'

'Oh, yes? We met once, did you say?'

'Yes, sir. I think you and Mrs Ffyrst were on holiday ... the West Indies, I think.'

'That was the summer Bernard graduated, he sat our house for us, had a couple of friends with him. They were departing as we returned ... a man and woman ... with a Land Rover.'

'That was me, sir.'

'Well, bless my soul. What can I do for you?'

'I'm trying to trace Bernard. I wonder if you could help me?'

'I think I could. Wouldn't give out his

home number over the phone – you could be anybody, and still less would I give out an address.'

'Of course.'

'But I don't see why you can't have his mobile number. Can't see how that can compromise him.'

'Very good of you, sir.' Paul Stapylton wrote down Bernard Ffyrst's mobile phone number.

Stapylton replaced the receiver, picked it up again and then replaced it again. He reached for his own mobile and walked into the garden at the rear of his house. He walked to the sunhouse and sat in it, out of sight of his wife, of whom he had learned that she missed little and noticed much. He switched on the phone and dialled the number that had been provided for him by Aaron Ffyrst.

'Hello?' said a voice in Paul Stapylton's ear. In the background, he could hear the hum of conversation and soft music.

'Bernard?'

'Yes ... who's this?'

'Paul Stapylton.'

A pause.

'Paul...?'

'Where are you?'

'In a bar in a hotel in Sheffield.'

161

'Sheffield?'

'Yes. Sheffield. I never thought I'd hear from you again.'

'Likewise.'

'So, where are you?'

'At home, near Wetherby. You've seen the papers?'

'When do I get time to read the papers? No, I haven't. Why? Haven't caught the TV news either. My gin is getting cold.'

'We have to meet.'

'We do?'

'Yes. We do. You remember the last thing you and I and Margaret Tennyson did together?'

Another longer pause.

'In the merrie greene woode?' Stapylton prompted.

'Yes?'

'Well, if you had caught the news, you'll have heard that our mutual has been found. His remains have anyway.'

'Oh no ... oh no ... oh no.'

'Oh yes, oh yes, oh yes. Margaret contacted me and we spent the afternoon together then went to the wood, big hole in the ground right where we planted Norris. Margaret's all for buckling, all for going to the police and coughing to everything.'

'She can't do that ...'

'Oh, but she can. Are you free to talk?'

'No, I'm with a colleague.' Then he added, clearly for the benefit of said colleague. 'It's my housekeeper.'

'I see ... look, call when you can.'

'It'll be tomorrow lunchtime now, Mrs Moore.'

'That'll do. Margaret won't do anything for a day or two, she's frightened of the consequences for her family; doctor's wife, three teenagers. Call me at work, Stapylton's Micro Engineering, York. It's in the Yellow Pages or Directory Enquiries.'

The Suicide Pilot liked working for Paul. Didn't know the man's second name, just Paul. Paul with the roller. Paul wanted someone taking care of, Paul would phone Mad Man Sean the Suicide Pilot ... point the guy out, or the woman, leave him at it ... no time pressure. Whether the person lived or died didn't matter so long as he was sorted. No reason was ever given. A length of three-eighths chain and a fractured skull sorted anybody. Then a hand delivered brown envelope was pushed through his letterbox, one thousand smackers. Enough for all the booze, all the junk ...

The room swayed. He held on to the brass rail which ran round the bar.

163

'You've had enough, Sean.' The landlord took his glass away. It was empty, but he'd be refused another.

Mad Sean nodded. He didn't want to give trouble. He liked this pub. He didn't want to be 'scratched'. But the pub was near ... clean ... comfortable ... his terraced house wasn't. His little house behind the railway station, the sheets on the bed he hadn't changed since ... the ashtrays he hadn't emptied since ... He held on to the bar rail to stop himself from falling, steadied and then over concentrating, and as if on automatic, walked to the door, into the street and home.

Five

In which George Hennessey meets a cleric, his mind turns upon the other tragedy in his life, and the gentle reader is introduced to his delight.

WEDNESDAY

'My parents, for example, were both doctors. Sugar?'

'No, thanks,' Hennessey and Yellich replied in unison.

'I think that they were a little disappointed that I didn't take a medical degree, but the vocation wasn't there. But they fully understood this.' He tapped his clerical collar. 'They are both practising Christians themselves, you see.'

'I see.' Hennessey extended his hand and accepted the mug of tea. 'Thank you.'

Yellich also accepted a mug of tea, thanking the Reverend Simon James. He sat with

165

Hennessey and Mr James at the heavy, dark-stained table, in the kitchen of the vicarage of St Michael and All Angels, Harrogate. The building, which Hennessey thought dated from the mid-nineteenth century, had a generous garden, as viewed from the kitchen window. A group of teenagers sat in a circle on the lawn, talking to each other. Hennessey was disappointed that he found himself surprised that the teenagers weren't smoking, or doing drugs, or drinking fortified wine, or selling their bodies. He'd clearly been a police officer for too long, if he was surprised that teenagers could be responsible and show self-respect and said so.

Hennessey and Yellich had left Micklegate Bar Police Station at nine a.m. that day, after a coffee without which the working day just would not start, and had driven to Ripon, via Harrogate, to the home of Simon James as recorded in Norris Smith's address book. The address, found easily upon a single set of clear instructions given by a cheery postman in a blue shirt, revealed itself to be a rambling Edwardian building, heavily encased in Virginia creeper which, at that time of the year, was in full bloom, a striking deep red against the lighter coloured brick, and a magnificent splash of colour between the green lawn in the foreground and the blue sky above. Hennessey and Yellich got out of their car and walked up to the front door and pulled a metal ring set in the door frame. They heard bells jangle and echo in a hallway.

The door was opened swiftly upon the ringing of the bell by a slight-built woman in a maid's uniform. She looked nervous at the sight of the two serious-looking strangers at the door.

'Police.' Hennessey smiled as reassuring a smile as he could.

'Yes ... yes...'

'Dr James, please.' He showed the maid his ID.

'Mistress doctor or master doctor?'

'Ah ... well, either actually.'

'If you'd care to step into the hall, sirs.' Hennessey and Yellich stepped into the cool shade of the hallway. Tall and narrow, it was panelled from floor to ceiling, and the ceiling was of ornate plaster. The maid walked to the rear of the house and out of the small door at the other end of the hallway. She returned a moment later and asked Hennessey and Yellich to 'come this way please, sirs'.

The officers were led through the house to the rear garden which seemed to both officers to be of park-like proportions, with landscaped borders, a large pond offset to the right, at the far end of which stood four magnificent beech trees, clearly much older than the house, yet planted in a line by human hand, and the garden too seemed to have a maturity which was older than the house. The only inference that Hennessey could draw was that 'The Beeches' had been built on the site of an earlier, possibly Georgian, house going by the age of the trees from which the building clearly drew its name, but the Georgian garden had been retained. Master doctor and mistress doctor walked towards the two officers from different parts of the garden, but both in gardening clothing, corduroy trousers, cotton shirts, stout shoes and wide-brimmed hats, gloves, each carrying a trowel. They walked confidently to the officers, smiling as they approached.

'Police?' the man said. 'How can we help?'

'Nothing to be alarmed about, sir, madam,' Hennessey said.

'Thank you, Betty,' said the lady of the house and in a manner befitting the house and its era, the maid gave a slight curtsey and walked silently back inside the house.

'We're trying to trace your son, Simon. This was given to us as his last address.'

'Was it? Well I can tell you that your information is well out of date.' Doctor James was a tall, silvery-haired man but a man clearly of good health for his age which Hennessey thought must be at least seventy years. His wife, too, was of similar age, and in similar good health. They were a couple who were clearly very happy to be an item. He was pleased for them. They reminded him of a middle-aged couple he had once encountered running a health food shop, the healthy complexion, the alertness in the eyes, the supple body movements. 'I hope he's not in trouble?'

'Not at all, sir, but he may hold information.'

'Helping with inquiries, love that phrase. Well our son is now a minister of the Church of England. He has an incumbency in Harrogate.'

'Oh...' Hennessey smiled, 'we drove through Harrogate on our way here.'

'Well, that's where he is. He did his curacy in Toxteth, Liverpool 8, and I think that opened his eyes. But the church can't have a naive clergy. Naivety gets rooted out early on, naivety won't get you through theological college.'

'I can imagine.'

'The church tests you, makes sure that

you're made of the right stuff. It's not a calling for everybody and it's not an easy ride. So Simon ... Church of St Michael's and All Angels, Harrogate. The vicarage is the building next to the church itself.'

With Yellich again at the wheel, for George Hennessey, with good personal reason, had a distaste for motor vehicles and saw them as an unfortunate necessity of twenty-first century living, the two officers retraced their pleasant journey through rural north Yorkshire; a landscape of rich, fertile soil, woodland amongst the fields, undulating pleasantly with the occasional craggy, rocky outcrop to remind one that this was, after all, still Yorkshire and Wuthering Heights was but a short drive to the west.

'This will be as far as we get, boss.'

'You think so?' Hennessey turned and smiled at the younger man.

'Can't see how we can take it any further ... twenty years, boss. All right it's a murder, but the time gap ... and we know Simon James was in the States when it happened.'

'Never say die, Yellich. We said we'll take it as far as we can, so we'll do that. See how far we get.'

'Very good, boss.'

The journey continued in silence.

In Harrogate, after another enquiry for

directions, this time from a uniformed police constable, who seemed to recognise CID officers but who made no comment, the church of St Michael and All Angels and its vicarage were located with ease.

The vicarage door was opened as they approached. 'My parents phoned to tell me that you were on your way here.' Simon James was a tall man, like his father, but with black hair and a round face. He seemed to Hennessey to be a man fulfilled. 'I think that I can guess what it's about.'

'You can?'

'Norris Smith? I heard the news.'

'Quite correct.'

'I think you'd better come in.'

In the kitchen of the vicarage, sitting at the long wooden table, each man holding a mug of tea, Simon James said, 'So, Norris. Well, it wasn't easy for him. He hadn't the background. The law faculty of any university is the same – children of professional parents, lawyers in the main, private education rather than public sector in the main, so Norris was handicapped right from the start and, to top it all, he hadn't got any perceptible personality. He also wasn't up to the course. He had nothing to offer that made him acceptable, but had a yearning to be liked and accepted.'

'Which we all need.' Hennessey sipped his tea.

'Up to a point, and with considerable qualification.' Simon James smiled. 'No company is better than the wrong company, so I tell my children. And there are people whose rejection of me and dislike of me cause me to sleep at night.'

'Point taken.'

'The place Norris occupied on a very expensive course at the government's expense, because he got a generous grant, was wasted. Simple as that. If he had been naturally brilliant and played the local boy made good, then he would have won acceptance, but he hadn't the social skills. If the law faculty wanted someone to cause a social mix on the course which is fair enough, they could have made a better choice, for Norris's sake as well, because all it gave him was a significant failure in his life, and we all need achievement. Now *that* is what we all need.'

'Agreed on that point.'

'It was a function of the British class system, which is still with us and always will be, I'm afraid. So the people on that course year were sons and daughters of lawyers, of senior civil servants, very senior clergymen, doctors, as in my case, and I recall some very pukka surnames amongst our year group. Off the top of my head ... Collingwood, Howe, Goodchild, Purcell, Stapylton, Cockburn, spelled "Cock-burn" but pronounced "Co-burn".'

'Of course.'

'Campion, Pepys, Tennyson ... I could go on, but you get the impression.'

'We get the impression.'

'And the schools that had been attended; Eton, Cheltenham Ladies, Winchester, Glenalmond, Bradford Girls Grammar, Leeds Grammar, all well represented, plus a few minor public schools and other more obscure grammar schools, and in the middle of all that was Norris, with a surname like Smith, an education at a secondary modern school, a penchant for beer and black pudding and liver and onions and parents who kept a B&B called "Seaview". But he had a sincerity and an honesty that I liked. Others didn't seem to see that. And an integrity about him. I saw that in him as well.'

'I see,' Hennessey nodded.

'No aspect to his personality,' Simon James continued. 'That's what he needed, really an aspect, something to offer, something to talk about. What I mean is that one bloke on the course was a keen yachtsman, joined the sailing club; another was an out of doors type and went away each weekend with the Climbing Club; another was a film buff, another wanted her degree to be an entry into the Armed Services and spent each weekend with the Cadet Corps. And Norris, all Norris could do was drink beer, which he did in large quantities for such a small man. Comfort drinking, I believe, looking back.' Simon James paused. 'And we all spoke about our careers. Not all of us wanted to practise law, as in the case of Sandra Purcell, she successfully applied for the army. She knew what she wanted to do. I joined the clergy. That leaning was in me at university, in fact by the time the third year began I knew where I was being called to go. Others did practise, they're now solicitors, or mid-ranking barristers on their way to the bench.'

'The bench?' asked Yellich.

'Becoming a judge.'

'Ah.'

'But Norris didn't seem to have any ambition at all.'

'I'm beginning to see him,' Hennessey said. 'Not a good time for him.'

'A very bad time. He was deeply unhappy there.'

'But he got a degree? He left with something.'

'A pass degree. It was the final rejection. If they had failed him, he would have been allowed re-sits, but a pass degree is basically a certificate of attendance. It won't open any doors, like a good second or a first will. A pass degree is a dismissal. And then Norris's appearance wasn't up to much, short, balding, slightly protruding teeth in the middle of a bunch of people whose classical good looks were the result of generations of selective breeding. On every level, he was isolated on the course.'

'It's a wonder he stuck it, by all accounts.'

'I found myself taking him under my wing. What acceptance he did enjoy came about because I was part of the group, and he was seen as a friend of mine, sort of acceptance by proxy, if you like.'

'To the point of protecting him?'

'Probably.' Simon James pursed his lips. 'Probably I did. Not from physical harm as such, but from verbal and emotional hostility. A lot of people wanted to go to Oxford or Cambridge, didn't make it. York was good enough, excellent university, my first choice in fact, but for those who wanted "Oxbridge" then having to sit with Norris from Bridlington in lectures and tutorials seemed to compound their sense of failure and he bore the brunt of their resentment. He was the embodiment of their disappointment, and he got it from all sides.' James paused. 'One bloke, Bernard, the amazingly named Bernard Ffyrst, you see that's another classy name, not just "Bernard" but "Ffyrst", double "f" and a "y", not an "i", if you please. Germanic in terms of origin, so Bernard claimed. Now he really had it in for Norris. Status was important for Bernard, he was one of the ones who had a vision of himself studying amid the dreaming spires or punting in a straw boater on the Cam after the May balls, and so York was second best for him. He was a hugely built bloke, nearly twice as tall as Norris and probably three times his weight ... he really resented Norris, never let up on him from Day One.'

'Really?' Hennessey glanced at Yellich. 'Ffyrst, did you say?'

'Yes,' James smiled. 'Bernard Ffyrst. Why, is that significant?'

'Probably.'

'His father is, or at least was, a solicitor in York. The firm of Ffyrst, Tend & Byrd, and that was another of Bernard's problems, he was utterly under the thumb of his father. His father was what is now known as a "control freak" and dominated Bernard's life, kept him on a tight reign. Bernard went to a boarding school, but one in York, hoped to get away from his father by winning a place at "Oxbridge" which his father would have accepted, but he didn't make it, and went to York on his father's insistence. He always gave me the impression that he was a walking time bomb, waiting to explode out from under that repression. I was present when Bernard first saw Norris, in a tutorial. We were asked to introduce each other, say a little about ourselves, and Bernard's face, livid, red with fury that not only had he not made it to Oxbridge to get away from Ffyrst senior, but he had to sit in tutorials with little Norris Smith from Bridlington. Frankly, I thought it did Bernard good, but it meant Norris had a hard time of it.'

'Are you going to take your own advice?' Stapylton raised his eyebrows.
  'Meaning?'
  'Playing with a straight bat?'
  'No,' Ffyrst smiled. He was still the tall, hugely built man that Stapylton recalled from their heady university days, but the years had been good to him. He hadn't aged as much as Stapylton had thought he would have aged, and the Law, too, had been good to him. He looked like a man who not only

enjoyed, but was well accustomed to a good standard of living, the cut of his suit, the ample waistline. 'No. I don't think so.' His expression hardened again. The smile transitory, and brief. 'You see, I'm not bang to rights except by Margaret what's-her-name...'

'South.'

'Except by her evidence. You're not either. It's a difficult case for them to prove. If we keep our mouths shut, if we all keep our mouths shut, and that especially means Margaret, it's pretty well impossible for them to prove.'

'Pretty well?' Stapylton leaned on his car and allowed his eyes to be drawn to the pale skinned boy of about seventeen who had arrived with Bernard Ffyrst and who had then been dismissed to the far end of the lay-by, well out of earshot, by Ffyrst. At that moment the boy looked disconsolate and smoked a cigarette as much for something to do, it seemed, to Stapylton as it was for the enjoyment of the nicotine.

'She's the only link.' Bernard Fyrst's voice rose as an articulated lorry rumbled past. 'And she's got as much to lose as we have. It doesn't matter how much her conscience plagues her, she won't talk.'

'I wouldn't dismiss her, she's tortured,

she's got religion, she's overcome with guilt, even though she didn't do anything.'

'She did do something. She very definitely did do something, and you did. Perverting the course of justice is not a minor offence. You're both looking at ten years. I'll do life. I'm at a critical point in my career, five years good, hard work and I'm looking at the bench, Mr Justice Ffyrst. Even my father will be pleased with that. The alternative is ruin ... financial ruin, my name, my family name ... there have been one or two crooked solicitors exposed down the years, and once a retired judge was sent to prison for a few weeks for a repeated motoring offence, but I do not want to be remembered in the annals of the English justice system as the first barrister to be convicted of murder. And what about you?' Bernard Ffyrst nodded to Stapylton's Rolls Royce. 'I thought I was doing well with my BMW.' He patted the bonnet of the car on which he leaned. 'Confess to more than a twinge of envy when I saw you arrive in that thing, half expected to see you behind the wheel of the Green Goddess with long hair and a beard.'

Stapylton smiled. 'We've both done well. But my success is recent. Only in the last few years has the money rolled in. The good life is just beginning, me and number two wife are settled now. The boys took some time to accept her, she's nearer their age than mine.'

'A trophy wife?'

'I don't like that term. So ... did you marry?'

'No...' Ffyrst glanced at the cigarette-smoking boy. 'I never felt the need.'

'Which by compensation gives you a free reign in respect of your own proclivities.'

'So ... can't touch you for it.'

'Bang to rights, can't touch you for it ... you've picked up the patter all right.'

'Comes with the territory, old chum of mine. Comes with the territory.'

Cars, lorries, buses passed speedily in either direction. To a driver, or passenger, the occupants of the lay-by were two middle-aged men talking with each other, one leaning against the bonnet of a blue BMW, the other leaning against the bonnet of a maroon Rolls Royce. The third occupant of the lay-by would most probably be taken for a hitchhiker who, depressed at not getting a lift, had given up trying and had sat down on the grass verge. The road was the A661, Wetherby in one direction, Harrogate in the other. The rendezvous had been suggested by Stapylton, who knew the road, during a phone conversation he and Ffyrst had had that lunchtime. When they met for the first time in twenty-three years, it was five thirty p.m. and the traffic was the 'rush hour' traffic.

'So,' Stapylton brought the conversation back on track, 'what are we going to do? Margaret's going to the Law, I know she is. She's going to crack, she never was a tough nut. You mustn't dismiss her. You haven't spoken to her. I have.'

'OK, OK ... don't you start to panic, I don't need that. We've both got a lot to lose.'

'And all for the swing of a golf club. Why didn't you do that on a golf course, hit a little white thing into a small black hole. Why did you hit Norris's head instead?'

'Because it was there. It was there, sticking up from above the back of the chair, so inviting, the poxy little insect. I found myself with the club in my hand ... he shouldn't have been allowed on the course. If he'd gone to teacher training college like his brother ... he should have gone to a ... well, anywhere except university ... he was one of life's victims. Some people are serial victims, he was one.'

'Well, he was your victim. For three years. Why did you invite him to the house in the first place? We were all right, the three of us, your parents' huge house, a relaxing three weeks in the country before the start of the long grind until retirement. Why did you invite him?'

'I thought we needed someone to laugh at. I thought I'd show him what he was missing before sending him back to his parents' bed and breakfast thing. His little bedroom in the attic ... he told me about it once ... the racket the seagulls make, I wish I hadn't now...'

'But you did. I wish I hadn't collected him from the railway station with the Green Goddess, but I did.'

'I was surprised he accepted the invitation. He must have known he was going to be put down. Mind you, he needed putting down.'

'Not *that* far. Not that permanently,' Stapylton snapped.

'So what are we going to do? You really think Margaret Tennyson...'

'South.'

'Whatever. Do you think she'll go to the Law?'

'Certain of it. Today, tomorrow, next week, next month, next year, but she'll walk into a police station and say "I want to give information ... I want to report a murder". It's only a question of time.' Bernard Ffyrst looked about him, the rich fields of North

Yorkshire, a warm, early evening in the summer. 'Freedom, liberty,' he said quietly. 'Funny how you take it for granted, funny how you don't value it until you realise it could be taken from you.'

'It is, isn't it?' Stapylton followed Ffyrst's gaze across the meadowlands to the wide, low skyline, the blue above with white in the blue.

'And the privilege of being able to walk into a pub for a beer ... remember the nights in the Falcon Bearer?'

Ffyrst smiled. 'With Norris staying dry so he could get to drive the Goddess back to York?'

'Can't do much of that in the pokey.'

'Can't, can you?'

'Mind you, you'll be all right for one thing at least.' Stapylton nodded to the boy who was by then looking indignant at having been ignored for so long. 'But, me, I like the ladies.'

'I won't be all right for anything.' Ffyrst allowed an edge to creep into his voice. 'And what'll happen to your business if you go inside for ten years?'

'It'll disappear, my wife with it. The boys will go and live with number one wife in London. I'll come out to a life on the dole and hostel living, aged fifty-something.'

A pause.

A long pause. But each man knew what the other was thinking.

But for Stapylton there was more. There was that look of piercing collusion in the eyes of Bernard Ffyrst. He sensed once again his own will, his own personality being displaced by the will of Bernard Ffyrst. Once again, Stapylton was in the control of Bernard Ffyrst.

The colours seemed louder, brighter, more vibrant. The sharp corners of rooftops of the buildings were sharper, more clearly defined, somehow. She noticed details she had not seen before, stone life-sized cats on the walls of the buildings near Museum Street. She looked up and pondered the sky, wondering when she would see it again as a free woman. She had lost track of the law in respect of serious crimes, magistrates don't hear murder trials, and she didn't know what were current sentencing trends, but Conspiracy to Pervert the course of Justice, or Con, the Accessory and Abettors Act as amended, whatever she would be charged with, she could expect a prison sentence and, as she was once a magistrate of the Harrogate Bench, the judge would probably feel he would have to make an example of her.

She walked on, savouring the city. She turned into Davygate and walked past a street entertainer in a colourful costume who had won a large crowd, she walked past beggars in the doorways, young people with signs saying 'hungry, homeless, please help'. Often she noticed the beggars would have a puppy on the end of a piece of string, and, continuing to pull every trick in the book, many had cultivated a lost, helpless look about the eyes. She walked past buskers, some who plucked awkwardly on guitars, and sang pathetically, others who played clarinets or violins, rendering soul-uplifting, classical music with consummate skill. She felt the urge to lose herself in the snickel-ways at the end of Davygate. She found one, Hornpot Lane Nether, she noticed it was called, and turned into a narrow curved passage, in which there were three 'tunnels' and, as always, the narrow passage offered a sudden silence from the noise and the bustle in the main street. She followed the snickel-way back to Swinegate, and joined the throng once again. She walked into Lower Stonegate, narrow, medieval, and turned right into Stonegate itself at the end of which she caught site of the Minster.

The Minster.

She stared at it. It offered a solution. She walked towards it, crossed into Minster Gates, left into Minster Yard by the Roman column and was reminded of the often seen ghosts near the Minster; the column of Roman soldiers, and the little girl at a window of a house forcibly confined to die of thirst because her house had been visited by the plague, her parents having abandoned her after painting the sign of the plague, a yellow cross, on the door. So went the story. Both those ghost sites were at the far side of the Minster from where she walked.

She entered the building by the main entrance opposite Precenters' Court, noticing the new masonry above the door, blending sensitively with the old; the masons of the late twentieth century taking pride in demonstrating that they were as skilful as their medieval forbears. She walked to the centre of the building to light a candle. There were a few unlit candles left, she took one, took a pound coin from her purse and placed it in the tin, then waited whilst a young man in a University of Wisconsin T-shirt held his candle to the flame of another already burning candle. Once he had lit his candle and placed it on the rack, she stepped forward and did the same. She lit her candle for Norris.

Husband or no husband.

Children or no children.

Standing or no standing in the community.

She had always known what she must do, but now she knew she must do it sooner rather than later.

She exited the Minster at Minster Yard, and stepped once more into the sunlight which caused her to blink her eyes after the comforting gloom of the interior of the cathedral. She looked round her ... she laughed softly to herself, the ludicrousness of it – she, a magistrate who had sent people to prison, she an intelligent woman, a law graduate, a long-time resident of the city of York and its environs, and she didn't know where the police station was. To have to ask directions so as to turn herself in ... it was ... all she could do was laugh, but there was relief in the laughter ... she hadn't laughed at all about anything for a long time. She composed herself and sought someone to ask directions of.

Most people seemed to be tourists, many in groups, carrying cameras, though one lady didn't stare this way and that but looked straight ahead as she walked. She didn't carry a guide book or a shoulder bag slung round her neck, instead she carried plastic shopping bags from Marks & Spencer and, in a warm, local accent, she directed Margaret South to Micklegate Bar Police Station.

It was just too bad, she thought, too bad for Paul Stapylton and his at-last-booming-business, his much younger wife and his sons who are not ready to carry on the business, and it's especially too bad for Bernard Ffyrst, wherever he is now, because he tormented a human being for three years and rounded it all off by murdering him. Then he compounded the felony by condemning his victim's family to twenty years of emotional torture ... if one of her children had vanished ... and if for twenty years she didn't know ... As she walked, determination entered her stride and she began to place her feet one in front of the other with increasing strength, increasingly confident.

Then her mobile phone rang.

She stopped walking and stepped into a shop doorway, so as not to cause an obstruction. 'Hello,' she said, holding the neat device against her ear.

'It's Paul.'

'Paul...'

'Yes, where are you?'

'I'm...' she looked around her. 'I'm in ...

Feasgate. In the centre of York. Paul, I'm on my way to the police station. I've thought it over ... I'm going to make a statement ... I can't live like this ... it is a lie.'

'No. Don't. Not yet. I've contacted Bernard...'

'You have?'

'Yes. In fact he's with me right now. He has an idea.'

'Like his last idea? I'm not really interested, Paul.'

'We feel the same as you. No point in running any more. But it's going to be better for us if we all go together.'

'He's willing to do that?' Margaret South felt a flood of relief.

'Yes, yes he is. So wait, will you? You owe it to us.'

'I might owe it to you, Paul. I don't think I owe Bernard anything.'

'Whatever. But we want to play with a straight bat, full confession, throw ourselves at the mercy of the court.' Stapylton was insistent. 'I'll drive into York, pick you up, then we'll collect Bernard.'

'All right...' she paused. 'Yes, all right. Where shall I meet you?'

'The same place we last saw each other before the beginning of this week.'

'The railway station?'

'Yes. Seems appropriate, don't you think? There's something neat about it, meeting there has a neatness about it.'

'Yes...' she smiled with relief, 'there's something neat about it. I'll be there in about ten minutes. I'm pleased we're doing this, Paul. Very pleased. I'll call you when I get to the station.'

Commander Sharkey looked at Hennessey then at Yellich and then at Hennessey again. He broke the heavy silence in his office by saying, 'Tread carefully, George.'

'Yes, sir.'

'A felony is a felony is a felony and no one is above the law, but a barrister...'

'Long way to go before we have a case, sir ... all it is at present is a finger of suspicion ... but he was found buried in a wood which at the time of his death was owned by the father of someone in his year group at university. There's no link at all that will satisfy the Crown Prosecution Service, but like I said, myself and Sergeant Yellich thought it best to appraise you of where this inquiry is heading.'

'Yes, thank you for doing that. Keep it by the book, George. Keep it by the book.'

George Hennessey drove home. Slowly. He

drove home early that day, earlier than normal so as to avoid the rush hour. His position allowed him a certain latitude of timekeeping, but as he always, always, always, put in more hours than the thirty-seven and a half hours' weekly commitment his contract stipulated for which he did not claim overtime, an early finish was a rare and permissible bonus. He drove out of York on the A19 through Shipton, across flat countryside, and as he drove, he was suddenly overtaken by a motorcyclist, travelling at speed, hunched down over the fuel tank of the machine to reduce windage, a young man whom Hennessey thought didn't believe he could be killed, a young man who thought that death was something that came to others. The cemeteries, as it is oft said, are full of such as he. And then the pain came, as always, an arrow-like pain piercing his chest, a moment after the sight or sound which was the trigger for the memory, and he was suddenly back in Greenwich, in his parents' little terrace house in Colomb Street, off Trafalgar Road, at the bottom end, near the hospital, near Maze Hill. Not the top end of Trafalgar Road, the Naval Academy end, the Observatory end, but Greenwich nonetheless, where all local business call themselves after

191

Meridian: 'Meridian Café', 'Meridian Car Hire'.

Hennessey hadn't been back to the place of his childhood for many, many years. Now so long had he been away that he feared to return, the inevitable changes he thought he was sure to see would, he feared, be too much for him. It would be the loss of another anchor. The demolition of his school had been a strange loss of unforeseen consequences. It had been an old building and was knocked down to make way for a block of flats. It was after he had learned of its demolition that Hennessey felt suddenly cast adrift. School is an important part of any person's life, and he felt envious of those people, the great majority of people, who once or twice a year, or even once a decade, can visit their old school, to touch their roots.

He remembered Graham polishing his motorcycle, his beloved Triumph, his 'Silver Beauty', as he called her. Graham would take him for a spin, on Sunday afternoons, up to Trafalgar Square and back. Then one night, Graham had ridden off on his machine and George Hennessey had lain in bed listening to the sound of Graham's machine as it roared away down Trafalgar Road, towards the Cutty Sark and beyond.

Then he heard other sounds, the traffic, the ships on the river ... a drunk staggering underneath his window, slurring his 'Hail Mary's' in a heavy Irish accent. Then there was that chillingly soft yet authoritative tap on their front door, the police officer's knock. Tap, tap ... tap. A knock he would come to use. Then the soft voices, his mother's wailing, and later his father came to his room, fighting back tears to tell him that Graham had ridden to heaven 'to save a place for us'. And the funeral, in the summer, seemed so wrong then, and now when he was close to retirement, it still seemed so wrong that people should die in the summer time. It was so wrong to watch his brother's coffin being lowered into the ground, when butterflies fluttered by and birdsong filled the air. He also saw then that it is not the hole one fills that one is measured by, it's the hole that one leaves behind.

From that day, there had been a significant gap in George Hennessey's life. He no longer had an elder brother, older, wiser, someone to turn to, someone to follow. Hennessey watched the youth on the motorcycle speed away ahead of him and was relieved to see that he negotiated the bend in the road, leaning heavily as he did so and, once again, found it difficult to understand humankind's love affair with the most dangerous machine ever invented, whether two wheels or four.

He entered Easingwold, stopped at the grocer's shop for a carton of milk and then drove further down Thirsk Road to his house, and his heart leapt as he saw parked half on, half off the kerb, a familiar car. A very familiar car indeed.

'Tell me something,' Hennessey said, when fifteen minutes after arriving at his home, he and the younger man sat together on the patio sipping tea. 'Have you come across a barrister called Bernard Ffyrst?'

'Yes,' Charles Hennessey nodded. 'I know him, not well, but there aren't many of us so we get to know each other. Why is he defending someone you nicked?'

'Can't say. Mind you, I suppose he will be defending in a sense.' George Hennessey watched Oscar drop his bone and run barking at a wood pigeon that had the temerity to land on 'his' lawn. Having seen off the wood pigeon, he returned, tail wagging, to the bone.

'Sounds intriguing. He comes from a legal family. His father is a senior partner in Ffyrst, Tend & Byrd, known in the legal community as "First, second and third", but a reputable firm. They don't do criminal work, though, no money in Legal Aid briefs for murder cases. Bernard is a very imposing man, hugely built, quite the largest man among my acquaintances, and he uses his bulk to intimidate witnesses. He is a formidable prosecutor, utterly merciless, especially with timid defendants. Mind you, I suspect that he's like all bullies, if you stand up to him, he'll roll on his back with his arms and legs in the air wanting his tummy tickled. Have you met him?'

'Not yet.' George Hennessey sipped his tea. 'But what you say is interesting. Do you think he could be violent, physically speaking?'

'Yes, if only because we are all capable of violence, verbal violence, emotional violence and physical violence. I am, you are, and I dare say Bernard Ffyrst is.'

'But allowing for that, would you say he has a low threshold of self-control?'

'I couldn't say, Dad, I don't know him that well. He's not the sort of person I'd choose as a friend. Frankly, I don't care for him, he has a … well, his utter ruthlessness, a win-at-all-costs attitude, very careerist. He gets results, but legal principles and ethics don't seem to be at the forefront of his mind. There is, I find, an amorality about him which shines through, despite his lip service to the contrary.'

'I see. So what are you doing this week?'

'A murder at Teeside Crown Court. I'm going NG despite a myriad of witnesses for the Crown and my advice, but he says he didn't do it, and I have to act on my client's instructions. We finished our closing speeches to jury late in the day and the judge said he had no time to sum up, so we got off early. He'll sum up tomorrow, the jury will retire and speedily return a verdict of G, and the defendant will get "life". He should have pleaded guilty, he would still have collected his "life" sentence but his acceptance of his culpability would have meant an early parole.'

'I know the type. If they claim they didn't do it often and hard enough, they come to believe it themselves. Depressing, I find.'

'It is. How's the love life?'

'Very well, thanks, be going over there this evening. Feed and walk Oscar, then I'll go over.'

'When am I going to meet her?'

George Hennessey smiled. 'Whenever. When you meet, you meet, but we're not going to merge households, be far too complicated at our age. Besides which Jennifer's in the garden, and I won't leave her.'

'Couldn't have been easy for you, bringing me up on your own.'

'It wasn't but it was rewarding. I'd live those days again if I could.'

'I've got a wife to help me with mine, or rather I help her since she does the lion's share of it on a day-to-day basis, but a single parent with a tough job, I take my hat off to you.'

Charles Hennessey, having taken his leave, Oscar having been fed and walked and provided with sufficient food and water for the night, George packed an overnight bag and drove to Skelton, to the north of York, a pleasant village he always thought, with a delightful tenth-century church. He parked his car in the road in front of a mock-Tudor, half-timbered, detached house and walked up the gravel drive, the crunching of the stones announcing his arrival before his polite, reverential tap on the door.

Moments later, he sat at the long table in the kitchen of the house, enjoying a cup of mint tea. He and the lady looked into each other's eyes, smiling softly at each other, one of those moments between two people when silence says more than a thousand words. Above them, three children ran backwards and forwards along the corridor, 'shifting' themselves, using 'their' bathroom rather

197

than the other bathroom, which was for the adults' use.

Minutes elapsed and then silence descended. George Hennessey and the lady waited a few more minutes. Then Hennessey said, 'Well ... it's gone quite ... shall we go up?'

'Yes,' Louise D'Acre smiled even more warmly. 'We can go up now.'

Six

In which another wood gives up its dead, Yellich makes a house call and a link is established.

THURSDAY MORNING

The woman looked at the other woman. She saw that she was neatly dressed in clothing of good quality, not designer wear, but good solid, sensible High Street clothing. The jewellery was ... respectable. The woman thought that was the word – respectable. The watch wasn't Cartier, but wasn't mail-order either. The shoes were, like the clothing, solid and sensible. The woman sat upright, against a tree at the edge of the wood, very still. She seemed, by her clothing, to be middle-aged but it was actually difficult for the first woman to gauge the age of the second, not being able to see the head and the face. That source of information

199

wasn't available to her, her head being covered by a plastic bag.

There was no movement, no clawing at the bag, no desperate gasps which would be the case had there been life still left to be saved. The first woman pulled her dog gently by the lead and walked away, and looked for a phone box. She had an emergency call to make, she had a suicide, an apparent suicide, to report.

Louise D'Acre drove her Riley, slowly and sedately, out of York, following the directions that she had been given to the village of Linton-on-Ouse, to the north and west of the city. As she drove, her mind turned suddenly to her childhood, when her father drove the car, the only car he ever owned, with her mother in the front passenger seat, and her in the rear seat, a doll in her hands. Now the car was hers, red and white, circa 1947, 1500cc, wooden dashboard, leather seats which used to stick to her legs in the long summers of far-off days. Her father had bequeathed it to her, and she cherished it, never exceeding fifty miles an hour, and always braking gently, never harshly. It was cared for, equally lovingly, by the proprietor of the garage she patronised who had made her promise that, should she ever choose to

200

sell the vehicle, he would be offered first refusal. And she had given the promise but with the fair warning that since it was a family heirloom and that she intended in turn to bequeath it to her son, Daniel, then its sale to anyone was highly unlikely. That had been acceptable to the garage proprietor who proceeded to lavish tender care on the vehicle in the hope that one day it might, just might, belong to him.

Louise D'Acre drove into Linton-on-Ouse, through the village and to the country beyond the village and to where she saw police activity, the area car with the blue flashing light, the unmarked police car, the constables in white shirts and serge trousers. She halted the Riley behind a police car, opened the rear hinging door of the car and swivelled, ladylike, both legs together, out of the car and walked towards the constables and the reassuring presence of George Hennessey, and the younger DS Yellich. They nodded as she approached and Hennessey said, 'Good morning, Dr D'Acre.'

'Morning Inspector.' She was stern faced, very serious, pointedly so, because just a few hours earlier she and the Chief Inspector had taken breakfast together at her house and had driven away in their cars, he to his place of work, she to hers. 'This is getting to be a habit, meeting in woodland, in the environs of our city, having discovered deceased persons therein.'

'Two in one week.' Hennessey smiled grimly. 'This one is a little ... well, not so old, and, as you see, not buried. Dr Mann the police surgeon pronounced life extinct at...' He turned to Yellich. 'Nine fifteen a.m.' D'Acre consulted her wrist watch. It was nine fifty a.m. She glanced about her, flat fields, meadows, hedgerows, the wood, and the Ouse to their left at a distance of perhaps a quarter of a mile, sliding silently southwards towards York. 'She was found in that position, I take it, propped up against the tree?'

'She was. A lady who was walking her dog found her, and reported it. Why? Is the position of her body significant?'

'Oh, I think so.' Louise D'Acre smiled and caught eye contact with George Hennessey. 'I think it means your looking at murder.'

'Not suicide?'

'No, I wouldn't think so. When people take their own lives, there is always a death struggle, people who overdose will choke even in unconsciousness as their body rejects the poison. And in all suicides by asphyxia using a plastic bag that I have seen,

202

there has been an attempt to claw the bag away in a last-minute panic. Further, if this was a suicide, she would be lying on her side. Not propped up.'

'I see,' Hennessey murmured. 'Confess, I thought it had the stamp of suspicion about it. Leaving the jewellery, and the watch to give the impression of suicide. I'm too suspicious, I've been a cop for too long.' Louise D'Acre smiled at him. 'Nonsense, Chief Inspector. And a healthy cynicism is better than naivety. So tell me, how was the bag when the body was found? I mean, how did it look?'

'I didn't see it ... Yellich?'

'PC Pendleton was the first officer on the scene ... he's over there.' Yellich turned and with a slightly raised voice shouted. 'PC Pendleton!'

'Sir!' Pendleton detached himself from his fellow officers and ran at a trot to where Hennessey and Yellich and Dr D'Acre stood.

'You were the first to arrive at the scene, Constable?'

'First police officer, yes ma'am.' Pendleton was a young, eager officer, so thought Louise D'Acre. She also noticed an earnestness, a seriousness about the man.

'I don't want to suggest anything, or put

words into your mouth...' she shook her head and brushed a fly from her face, 'but can you describe the bag?'

'Ordinary bin liner, ma'am, black...'

'Yes.'

'Well, fully over her head, pulled down so that her head was at the end of the bag, the bag covered the shoulders...'

'Pulled right down?'

'Yes, ma'am.'

'Anything about the bag that struck you as noticeable?'

'No ... no...' Pendleton spoke slowly. 'No, it just hung limply.'

'Limply?'

'Yes, ma'am.'

'Now this is very important ... you used the word "limply" without any prompting from me?'

'Yes, ma'am.' A note of curiosity entered Pendleton's voice. Louise D'Acre smiled. 'Thank you, Constable.'

'Ma'am.' PC Pendleton turned and walked smartly back to join the other constables who stood by the roadside.

'I think that confirms it.' Louise D'Acre turned to Hennessey and Yellich, holding eye contact with one, then the other.

'It does?'

'You see, if the bag had been responsible

for her death, it would have been clinging to her face, she would have exhaled once with the bag in place and then upon inhalation, the bag would have compressed against her head due to the effect of atmospheric pressure, and it would be thusly held there, even if it did loosen over time, the impression of her face would be evident. Frankly, the constable's description is of a plastic bin liner being pulled down over the head of an already deceased person. A crude attempt to make it look like suicide.'

'So we *are* looking at murder?' Hennessey grimaced.

'I think so.' D'Acre spoke softly. 'I can't think of any other explanation. Can you?'

'I can't, to be honest.' Hennessey looked at the woman and, as the woman who found her, saw a middle-aged woman, who clearly enjoyed a pleasing standard of living, and where life had been cruelly cut short when she had many, many years of life ahead of her.

'I'll do the p.m., of course, but mouth and eyes open like that, no physical trauma that is evident, no disturbance to her clothing...' D'Acre paused. 'I would expect to find that she was murdered by having a plastic bag pulled over her head and then deposited here with another bag over her head.'

'Sometime in the night?'

'It would seem so.' D'Acre knelt by the corpse and felt the arm. 'Rigor is established but only just. No indication of decomposition. The condition of the body is consistent with death occurring within the last twelve hours ... possibly the last eighteen.' She stood again and her eye was caught by the movement of a white coveralled scene of crimes officer replacing the film in his camera. 'Any idea of her identity?'

'Not yet. Matter of time though, a woman, clearly middle years, married ... she will be missed very rapidly and reported as such by a responsible person.'

'Margaret South,' the man restrained his emotions. Anger rose up in him and form filling, he thought, did not at all help matters. 'S.O.U.T.H., South.'

'South,' the constable repeated the name. 'Margaret. Age?'

'Forty-four.'

'Forty-four.' The constable added the information to the 'mis per' referral form.

'Last seen?'

'Yesterday forenoon. Twenty-four hours ago. I phoned last night when she didn't come home, the officer I spoke to said that they don't take missing person reports in

the case of adults until the person concern-
ed has been missing for twenty-four hours.
Well, it's now twenty-four hours. More, in
fact.'

'Yes, sir ... Doctor South, and you have no
idea where she is?

'I already told you. No.' Dr South continued to restrain himself.

'Yes, sir. Just following procedures.'

'I was asked to provide a recent photograph...' Dr South opened his jacket and
took his wallet from his breast pocket. From
the wallet he took a photograph and handed
it to the constable. 'It's a good photograph
of her, a good likeness. She always did
photograph how she looked. You may have
noticed that some people don't look at all
like the photograph they take, but Margaret
always does. That snap is about a week old.
Couldn't get more recent.' He replaced his
wallet in his jacket pocket.

'Thank you, sir.' The constable attached
the photograph to the report with a paper
clip. 'Was Mrs South on foot when she left
the house yesterday?'

'No, she took her car. Red Mercedes.'
South gave the registration number.

The constable thanked Dr South for reporting his wife as a missing person and
advised him that 'an officer' would call on

him at his home. South nodded silently and walked out of Micklegate Bar Police Station, head down as if, thought the constable, a great weight had fallen on him, a weight that he couldn't shrug off and that he was doomed to carry. The police constable was young with only five years of police service to his name, but he was already developing a police officer's 'nose', and his 'nose' told him that South was 'OK', that South had not harmed his wife in any way. His 'nose' also told him that there was going to be a 'story' to this 'mis per', that he shouldn't just file it away once the procedurally required 'home visit' had been done following the initial report. There was something more to this one. He picked up the phone and phoned the collator, alerting him to the report.

Thomas South paced the floor of his living-room. His three children sat in the room, not interacting, each looking worried, pale of face, lost. The phone rang. South snatched it up. His children heard one side of the conversation. 'South ... yes ... that's my wife's car ... I reported her missing today ... that is Micklegate Bar Police Station ... Well yes, at that police station this morning ... heavens, do you people talk to each other? Talk about the left hand not knowing what the right hand is doing ... we're on tenterhooks here ... right.' He replaced the phone. 'They've found Mummy's car,' he told his children, 'the police. Well, they didn't find it, the staff at the multi-storey car park reported it. It was left overnight. They thought it might have been abandoned ... I mean stolen, then abandoned.'

'That doesn't sound good.' His eldest son looked at him, and then at his siblings. 'Doesn't sound good at all.'

'It sounds bad. Margaret...' He excused himself, managed to hold back his tears until he had locked himself in the bathroom.

Hennessey and Yellich returned to Micklegate Bar Police Station, signed in and checked their pigeonholes. Hennessey read the memo placed in his pigeonhole. He then handed it to Yellich. 'What do you make of that?'

'From the collator.' Yellich paraphrased aloud. 'Lady called South, reported missing ... forty-four years of age, her car was reported as having been abandoned overnight in a multi-storey ... car is a Mercedes Benz, husband Dr South...' He glanced at Hennessey. 'You know, skipper, I don't need to look at the photograph on the mis per file to tell you that Mrs South is no longer missing, her body isn't anyway.' He handed the memo back to Hennessey. 'I knew the Norris Smith inquiry would be buried by something.'

'I know,' Hennessey nodded. 'How many forty-four-year-old doctors' wives go missing in the Vale each year?'

'Not many, boss. No more than one a night. Do you want me to do it?'

'If you'd be so kind, Yellich, if you'd be so kind.'

One hour later DS Yellich and Thomas South stood in a dimly lit room which was softly yet substantially furnished with leather upholstered benches and wood panelling. Two heavy velvet curtains hung against one wall. Beside the curtain was a door.

'I usually tell people what...'

'Well, you don't have to tell me, Detective Sergeant. I know very well what I'm going to see.' He was a tall man, taller than Yellich.

The two men continued to stand in silence. The sound of a trolley was heard beyond the curtains, a soft 'click' as the metal brushed against the wall, a squeaking of a wheel. South grimaced and said, 'Try as they might, they can't be completely silent.'

A few seconds later a nurse entered the room via the door beside the curtain. Her expression was solemn, very solemn. She looked at Yellich who nodded. The nurse pulled a cord and revealed a large glass screen and beyond that the body of the woman who earlier that day had been found propped up against a tree just outside the village of Linton-on-Ouse. The body was now tightly wrapped in starched white linen, tucked in tightly under the mattress of the trolley, and the head wrapped in bandages so that only the face was visible. By some trick of light and shade, it looked as though it was floating in a black void.

'Yes...' Thomas South nodded. 'That is my wife, Margaret South.'

'Thank you, sir.' Yellich nodded once again to the nurse who pulled the cord and closed the curtains.

Three quarters of an hour later DS Yellich and Thomas South stood in another, more spacious room, a room flooded with natural light, courtesy of French windows which looked out on to a large lawn on which a badminton court had been painted and a net hung. The room was painted in light blue pastel, with a light grey carpet and light grey, deeply upholstered furniture. A modern art painting, a bold, striking bolt of red against a field of various shades of green, which to Yellich's untrained eye looked to be an original, hung over the fireplace. The South children being at the moment comforted in the house of a sympathetic neighbour, Yellich and Thomas South were at liberty to speak.

'I'm sorry to have to question you, Dr South ... but the first twenty-four hours of a murder investigation are crucial.'

'I can understand that.' South poured a whiskey from a cut glass decanter. 'Do you...?' He held up the decanter.

'No, thank you, sir. Not on duty.'

'You don't mind if I...?'

'Not at all.'

South poured a stiff whiskey, a generous measure which he didn't dilute. 'I'm not a good doctor you know ... well, I deliver, I come up with the goods, no complaints ... but I'm the original hypocrite. I warn against the demon drink ... half a dozen patients in each surgery I should think, come home and ... this.'

'I'd do the same if I were you, sir. I mean at a time like this ... and alcohol has its place.'

'Religious ceremony and the pubs being central to working-class culture, you mean?

212

Yes, I dare say it has.'

'And I confess that I subscribe to the notion that an alcoholic is someone who drinks more than his doctor. I have the misfortune to be on the list of a teetotal GP and even if I drink a half pint of beer and am unwise enough to tell him, I earn myself a most stern rebuke.'

South smiled. 'An alcoholic is someone who drinks more than his doctor. I'll remember that.' He sipped the whiskey. 'But medicine is highly stressed, it's a position which carries status but we pay a price for said status.' He paused. 'We once had a partner in our practice who took pills and bottles from our dispensary and placed them on a table in the waiting room with a sign inviting the patients to help themselves because, he said, that method of distributing medicine was no more random that the prescription method. He'd had enough you see, he took an early retirement before he broke down completely.'

Another large pause. 'Well, thank you for interjecting humour, ease the atmosphere ... you're good at your job, Mr Yellich. So shall we address the matter in hand? And the answer is "no", I don't.'

'Don't what, sir?'

'Know of anyone who would want to harm

my wife. That was going to be your first question, was it not?'

'It was.'

'Well that's your answer.' South sat in an armchair. 'Please...' he indicated a second armchair of such cavernous proportions that when Yellich accepted the invitation to have a seat, he felt it to be more like the chair was swallowing him than it felt as if he was sitting in it.

'Can you point us in the right direction? She disappeared ... you reported her missing ... anything unusual happen of late?'

'Well...' South looked at the ceiling, then at the carpet. The phone rang in the hall. South said, 'It's all right, the answermachine will catch it.' The two men listened to the phone ring, then the answermachine's recording. 'You've reached the South household, we can't take your call at present, if you leave a message we'll call you back' then a loud "beep" then a male voice said 'Tom, it's Lionel ... hope all is well.' The machine clicked and whirred. South glanced at his watch. 'That time already. That's Lionel Tutt, one of the partners. Morning surgery must be over ... he wouldn't phone during surgery hours. So your question, well, yes, whether it's relevant or not I don't know but Margaret has been a different woman for the last few weeks. Not herself at all.'

'Oh?'

'She was preoccupied, clearly there was something on her mind. Margaret was a woman of high moral scruples. She wouldn't do anything that was unethical, even if it was legal. And earlier this year she resigned from the Harrogate Bench. She used to be a magistrate.'

'I see.'

'She wouldn't say why she resigned, but it wasn't because of an issue involving the Harrogate Bench, so I can only assume that it was personal, deeply so, otherwise she would have confided in me. I asked her what it was that was eating her up from the inside, but she wouldn't tell me. We had this rule, a thing about communication, it makes ... it made our marriage successful ... it made our relationship work. No secrets. Just two simple words but we meant it, and observed it. It means that if Margaret was keeping something from me, it could only have been to protect me and the children rather than that she was keeping me in the dark. And I believe she would have told me what "it" was eventually.'

'I'm beginning to see what sort of lady she was.'

'One day fulfilled and realising it, a

wonderful centre of family life, an excellent mother to our children, then a withdrawn, distant woman. And nothing happened in the house, no argument with me, no problem with our children ... she even gave up helping in the charity shop. She helped out to get herself away from the house for a few hours a day.'

'Something highly personal?' Yellich said. 'Something she couldn't talk even to her husband about. Something from or in your wife's past?'

'Confess that has occurred to me. Didn't want to suggest it but it's the only explanation.' He drank deeply of the whiskey. 'It has to be, hasn't it? It's not from her future. That's not a silly thing to say because I believe in premonition and also because stupid people have ruined their lives by going to fortune-tellers and have come away believing in a bad prophecy, and made it come true by believing it. A self-fulfilling prophecy I believe it's called. Margaret didn't go to fortune-tellers and if she had had a premonition she would have told me.'

'And it's nothing in her present?'

'No. No marriage problems, no money problems, no family problems, no health problems, yet for weeks she is a troubled woman, then she disappears and is found murdered. It has to be something from her past.'

'It looks that way.'

'And it's something from her deep past, possibly from before we were married because nothing has happened within the years of our marriage that could haunt her.'

'So, let's go back,' Yellich suggested. 'Tell me about her, her life before you became involved with each other.'

'What I know...' South drained the glass and laid it down heavily on the table beside the chair. 'Margaret came from Sussex, her father was a senior minister in the Anglican Church, a bishop ... died a few years ago ... her mother is still alive ... I'll have to tell her ... that won't be easy. We met here, at York, both students at the university. I read medicine, of course, she was a lawyer. I come from Sunderland so we met halfway and stayed. It was a good twenty years, the practice was pleasant to work in, the doctors, the nurses, the practice manager, all formed up and settled down into a very settled team. I loved going to work, I loved coming home, the children, Margaret, now this ... I knew it would end, but not like this ... not so soon. I still can't take it in. You know, when I was a boy, like all children I'd complain that something "wasn't fair" and my parents would retort and say "life's not fair". As a doctor, I see a lot of life's unfairness, birth deformities, children with cancer, horrific injuries in the prime of life, which make you realise that sometimes it's better to be lucky dead than dead lucky. But the essential unfairness of life didn't reach me, not until now, a widower at my age. The lesson's been a long time in coming but it's come and my parents were right.' Thomas South stood and poured himself another whiskey of such generous proportions that it made Yellich wince at the thought of having to drink it. 'You know, this is in your interests...' South turned stiffly and swayed back to the armchair and sat heavily, nearly spilling his drink. 'A drunken suspect ... *in vino veritas* ... might let something slip out.'

'Should you be a suspect?'

'Of course. What's that you say "before you look at the outlaws, always look at the in-laws"? Stranger crime is far more infrequent than relate ... relationship crime ... so I'm a suspect.' He held up his glass. 'Sure you won't join me ... a little one ... keep me company, I've got a lonely road ahead of me now.'

'No,' said Yellich firmly, not at all suspecting that South had anything to do with his wife's murder, reasoning that if he had, then he wouldn't lower his shield by drinking, but if truth was emerging in the alcohol, it was to reveal Thomas South as a needy person and a selfish one. The unfairness of *his* life, *his* lonely road...

'Well I left for work yesterday, surgery in the forenoon, rounds later on in the day, witnesses aplenty. Got home about five thirty, children were here but no Margaret. That was strange, Margaret's always home when I get home, holding the household together. I phoned round friends and other places she might be, no one knew of her whereabouts. There was a message on our answermachine, a family friend who is sensible and courteous enough always to say what time and what date ... "this is Harry phoning on the morning of x at ten a.m." ... and the message on the machine was placed by Harry at ten fifteen. So it's safe to assume that Margaret had left the house before then. At ten p.m. last night I phoned the police to report her missing. They wouldn't accept the report, they told me they can't accept a mis per report as they called it unless the person had been missing for twenty-four hours.'

'That's the procedure.'

'So I reported her at ten a.m. this day. An hour later, I was looking at her body. What an experience for a man to have.'

'We're getting off the track.' Yellich sensed the need to shift the focus from Thomas South. He also sensed it wouldn't be easy. 'Where were we?'

'Students, heady day ... ah yes ... I'd been around the block a few times but I was the only man Margaret ever "knew" in the biblical sense of the word. That also kept our marriage strong. Margaret took her law degree but never practised, never went into the Law. She socialised with the medics more than the lawyers, staid group the lawyers, but the medics are always the wildest bunch at any university. Once a couple of blokes and I stripped naked, ran a few hundred yards down the street to a students' pub, had a beer and ran back. The landlord laughed his socks off, understood the culture of his pub. The people in the pub laughed and cheered. Then we ran back down the street to our lodgings. But the lawyers ... smug, restrained ... I recall one of her friends, a huge guy ... rejoiced in the name of Bernard. Bernard Ffyrst ... first by name, first by nature ... me, me, me.'

'Really?' Yellich's ears pricked up.

'Yes really.' Thomas South took a large mouthful of whiskey. 'Went to a party with Margaret once, a lawyers' party, all very proper, all well on their way to becoming High Court Judges and leading barristers, scoring points off each other, and in the middle of it was this little oik of a guy, blond haired, slightly bucktoothed, he was the butt of their humour. Margaret didn't patronise him, I liked her for that, but the others did. We'd only just become an item by then and I really liked her for that. I don't like bullying. She didn't bully him, but that Ffyrst guy, he wouldn't let up on the little blond-haired guy.'

'Recall his name, the short, blond guy?'

'Don't. Never saw him after that. Margaret said he was out of his depth, though. I remember that. All the other law students had professional middle-class parents. His parents kept a bed and breakfast on the Yorkshire coast somewhere. Why? Is it relevant?'

'Could be,' said Yellich. 'It could very well be.'

Seven

In which Hennessey learns of mechanical asphyxia and he and Yellich close upon the prime suspect.

THURSDAY AFTERNOON

The memory of the man came flooding back. Hennessey hadn't thought of the man for a number of years, but occasionally he would spring to mind. The memory of him would flash in and then out of his mind in a millisecond, and this was one such occasion. The man had been a mortuary assistant but unlike many other mortuary assistants, he had let his job reach him. When Hennessey knew him, the mortuary assistant was middle-aged and lived with his wife in a terraced house in Greenwich, close to Hennessey's parents' house. He was employed in the local hospital. He had to do the job, he was too old for a career move,

222

and he was terrified of dying. It was not that he saw dead bodies aplenty during his working hours, but that he knew that, should he die unexpectedly by accident or natural causes, he knew which stainless steel dissecting table his body would be placed on, which hands would remove his clothing, which hands would pick up which tool to saw into which part of his flesh. The man's every waking minute was one of sheer terror. He wouldn't go out of doors, even to collect a bucket of coal from the shed, or walk to the corner shops unless accompanied by his long-suffering wife, lest he trip and fall or forget his kerb drill and walk in front of a bus. Hennessey thought of the man then forgot him again: the matter in hand was pressing. 'That's interesting,' he said.

'I mean, a dreadful struggle is mild.' Louise D'Acre sat at her desk and glanced over the notes that had been typed up following her verbal account of the post-mortem. 'She was a woman who wanted to live all right, not one of her fingernails is not broken to a greater or lesser extent. Under each of her nails is not just blood, but slivers of skin, the scrapings have been placed in a productions jar. You'll have no trouble identifying the suspect, his face will be shredded and, once identified, more than enough blood under the fingernails to obtain his DNA signature. A very safe conviction for you, Inspector.' Louise D'Acre took a felt-tip pen and wrote 'Margaret South' beside the word 'name' on the front of the file. 'I was waiting until she had been identified,' she said, 'better than writing a file number where the name should be, only to have to cross it out again. That makes a dreadful mess.'

'Could you please send the blood to Wetherby anyway?' Louise D'Acre glanced at him. 'Have you arrested somebody already?'

'No, but he may be on the DNA register because of a previous crime.' Louise D'Acre smiled at him. 'I'll get it off today.'

'Thanks. Any sign of sexual activity?'

'Oh, plenty. She'd given birth for one thing.'

Hennessey inclined his head. 'Point to you. But of a recent and criminal nature.'

'No indication. In fact I'd go as far as saying that there was no sexual violation.'

Hennessey leaned back in his chair and glanced round D'Acre's office; framed photographs of Danny her horse, of her children, Daniel, Fiona and Dianne, of her timber-framed house in Skelton. The photograph showed the window of the bedroom where last night he and she had lovingly coupled. 'So, she wasn't raped, it wasn't a sexual attack, it wasn't robbery, her jewellery and watch were not removed, but somebody wanted her murdered. Why?'

'Well that, Chief Inspector, is your department, not mine.'

'Sorry, thinking aloud. She was asphyxiated, you say?'

'Yes. Mechanical asphyxia is my finding as to the cause of death. Smothering to be specific. She wasn't strangled, nor did she choke on a blockage in her airways, nor was she asthmatic. Fortunately, whoever murdered Mrs South, fortunately for us I mean, put us on the right track by attempting to pass the death off as suicidal suffocation. Had the plastic bag been absent, then it would have thrown me for a while because it's often difficult to tell what caused death if the plastic bag is disposed of. But I would have got there eventually by a process of elimination. No injuries to the face, no petechiae in the eye, small blood spots which occur when a person is strangled. Eventually I would have concluded that the cause of death was mechanical asphyxia, and the blood and skin under her fingernails pretty well confirms it. There are bruises to her shoulders and back, circular, pressure bruises consistent with her being held down on a rough, hard surface. The plastic bag would have to have been held tightly round her though, once she exhaled, the force of atmospheric pressure would have held the bag to her nose and mouth. As she attempted to inhale, she would have drawn the bag tighter. She would have had nothing to exhale. She would become comatose within a matter of seconds caused by the build-up of carbon dioxide, brain death due to oxygen starvation in five minutes, actual morbidity within ten minutes. It's a recommended way of committing suicide.'

'Recommended?' Hennessey raised an eyebrow.

'Note what I said. I didn't say suicide is recommended, but if you are going to do it, then avoid mess and pain. Don't throw yourself under a lorry, or lay across a railway track and oblige someone to pick your body up, all bloody and splintered. Don't hang yourself, it could take five minutes of panic-filled consciousness before you succumb to insensibility. Don't jump because if you're going to do a good job of it, you'll be falling for two or three or four seconds and you can do a lot of thinking in a second or two. I mean, it's no good wanting to change your mind when you're halfway down.'

Hennessey smiled. He enjoyed Dr D'Acre's wit, and her common sense.

'But a plastic bag, very neat, efficient and probably not unenjoyable. The build-up of carbon dioxide would induce a state akin to "altered consciousness" as I believe it's called, and you would have a sensation of travelling vast distances over a long period of time.'

'But, in fact, it's all over in a matter of minutes of real time.'

'As you say, but a lot neater than slitting your wrists. I mean if the alternative is a terrible death from inoperable cancer, you can't choose whether you live or die, but you can still choose the how and when of it.'

'It's worth thinking about, but talking of the how and when of it, the "how" in this case is answered. What can you say of the "when"?'

Louise D'Acre smiled. 'You ought to know better than to ask that, Chief Inspector. I could refuse to answer that question. But...' She glanced at her notes. 'Well ... you saw the body yourself, not a trace of tissue putrefaction and the early summer, rigor established when we got there, so late last night ... covering myself ... from six p.m. to about two hours before we got there.'

'Two hours, despite the rigor?'

'Covering myself.' Again a wry smile. 'But what did puzzle me was the contents of her stomach, or rather the lack of contents. You see this was a very well-nourished middle-aged woman, clearly knew the value of nutrition and a healthy, balanced diet, excellent teeth. She would not have gone without food out of vanity, nor by her quality of clothing that I noticed, out of poverty, yet her stomach contained no food at all, only a little carbonised material which I think will prove to be toast if we took it to the lab.'

'Breakfast?'

'Is my interpretation also. So, no lunch, no evening meal, despite the fact that she was likely, likely I repeat, to have been alive when those meals would have been taken.'

'Held captive before being murdered? Denied food?'

'Is completely your department, Chief Inspector. She died in a sitting position, possibly, probably *the* position in which she was found. The lividity, the settling of the blood due to gravity is localised at the buttocks and the back of her legs. So murdered, propped up when still limp, but lifeless, and stiffened where she was left.'

'It implies her death was premeditated.' Hennessey thought aloud. 'If she was held against her will, as the lack of food indicates, then her murder was premeditated. That means there was a motive.'

'What do you know about her?'

'Nothing. Sergeant Yellich is visiting her husband, who reported her missing. He gave his name as Dr South which, if he is a medical man, would explain the well-nourished body and dental hygiene, but being a university town, he could equally be a doctor of ancient Greek.'

'As you say ... but these are my findings. Death by mechanical asphyxia, sometime between eighteen hundred hours yesterday and ... seven this forenoon. And an empty stomach for you to puzzle over.'

Hennessey made to say something but Louise D'Acre froze him with a stare. Hennessey nodded, thanked her for the information and left her office. Work is work is work. She laid down that rule, and she enforced it rigidly.

'This fella Ffyrst, skipper. He keeps popping up in all the wrong places.'

'Does, doesn't he?' Hennessey sat forward in his chair and raised his eyebrows at Yellich who sat back, legs crossed in the chair in front of Hennessey's desk. 'We need to do some recapping here. Can't do that without assistance.' He stood and crossed the floor of his office to where a small table stood in the corner, on which sat an electric kettle, mugs, coffee and powdered milk. A few moments later, each man was cradling a mug of steaming hot instant coffee in his hands. Hennessey said, 'So, Bernard Ffyrst? Your thoughts, Yellich.'

'Well, he was mentioned in connection with Norris Smith.'

'Yes.'

'Mr ... Dr South remembers him as a fellow law student of his wife's before they were married.'

'Yes ... and you mentioned Dr South remembering a law student in that group who sat at odds with the rest and gave an excellent description of Norris Smith as we have come to see him.'

'Those were my thoughts, too, boss. Far from eclipsing the Norris Smith inquiry, it looks as though the murder of Margaret South is linked to it.' Yellich stroked a closely shaved chin and glanced out of Hennessey's office window, the walls, the tourists ... the sun glinting off the windows of modern buildings.

'It has all the hallmarks of a conspiracy. So, Norris Smith, just graduated with an indifferent class of degree is murdered. He sustains a massive blow to the back of his head. He is reported missing, as he would be, and remains a mis per for in excess of twenty years until his body is discovered by a man with one of those dreadful detector things. It transpires that the wood in which he was buried is privately owned. It further transpires that when Norris Smith was buried, the wood was owned by a wealthy local solicitor by the name of Aaron Ffyrst.'

'Father of Bernard.'

'Who, of the group of law students, seemed to be the one who most had it in for Norris Smith, according to the Reverend James.'

'He's got some explaining to do, boss.'

'Has he?' Hennessey opened his palm. 'Has he? What has he got to explain? I follow your thinking, Yellich, I follow it clearly. I mean what you are saying is that Bernard Ffyrst whacked Norris Smith over the head and then possibly, with the help of others, buried him in his father's wood. Probably thinking a "Private Wood" sign nailed to a tree would keep folk at bay. Tactical error, though, because it linked him to the murder. But we can't go to court with that, CPS won't wear it. The link isn't strong enough.'

'Yet.' Yellich smiled.

'Good for you, Yellich. I like determination in an officer. Yet. It isn't strong enough. Yet. So, leaving aside Norris Smith's murder for a moment, let us consider Margaret South's. We can find out her maiden name easily and it will be equally easy to find out if she was in the same year group as Norris Smith, but for the moment, we'll assume she was.'

'Oh...' Yellich drew breath between his teeth. 'That's a very dangerous assumption, boss.'

Hennessey sat back. 'It is, isn't it? I'm losing my touch. Perhaps I really am ready to retire.'

'All it would take is two quick phone calls.'

'On you go.' Hennessey indicated the phone on his desk. Yellich consulted his notebook and dialled Dr South at home. He spoke, listened, and then said, 'Thank you, sir ... no, no progress to report.' He replaced the phone and said 'Tennyson, boss. In those days she was Margaret Tennyson.'

'Phoning the university now?'

'No, boss. It would take too long.' Yellich turned the pages of his notebook. 'I thought I'd try the Reverend James, he's a reliable source of information. He'd know whether or no, and I think that Tennyson was one of the names he mentioned when he was telling us what a middle-class bunch they were. Remember, a lot of classy names in the middle of which was little Norris Smith. And here we are...' He picked up the phone again, dialled, and Hennessey heard him say, 'Good afternoon, Reverend. DS Yellich here. We called yesterday, my boss and me. Reverend, can I ask you if one of the students in your year group was a woman called Margaret Tennyson? She was?' Yellich glanced at Hennessey. 'Thank you, sir. Nothing to report yet, but we're making progress. Good day, sir.' He replaced the phone. 'No assumption about it now, sir. Margaret South, née Tennyson, Bernard Ffyrst and Norris Smith were all students in the same year group in the law faculty at the University of York, twenty-plus years ago.'

'And now two are murdered, and the second to be murdered was murdered just four days after the discovery of the body of the first to be murdered. Smells like rotting fish.'

'Doesn't it, sir.'

'So, if the news of the discovery of Norris Smith's body triggered the conscience of somebody who witnessed his murder, and if that person let it be known that they intended to do the sensible thing and go to the police with their information?'

'Somebody like Margaret South?'

'Exactly. Then who would have a vested interest in preventing them?'

'The murderer of Norris Smith.'

'Again exactly, particularly since they are no longer twenty-something, but are now forty-something and at a critical phase in a glittering career.'

'Someone like Bernard Ffyrst you mean, boss? Going from being a senior barrister, earmarked for a judge even, to doing porridge on Durham E wing, that's quite a nosedive. It would make any man do a desperate thing. I think we should quiz him, boss.'

'I think we should too, and as soon as. Didn't tell you, but Margaret South went down fighting, blood under every fingernail. She shredded the face of whoever murdered her. The sample's gone to Wetherby.' Yellich smiled. 'Left a present for us. Well done her, I say. Do we know where Ffyrst lives?'

Bernard Ffyrst lived in a house which had been built in 1716. The stone engraving above the doorway said so. It was an expansive house, neat, large, the door was offset from centre, three windows on the ground floor to the left of the front door and four to the right. There was a first floor and a second floor, and above, a vaulted roof. In the apex of the roof was a clock, blue face, gold numerals, gold hands, very striking against the off-white colour of the stonework. Hennessey took in the image of the house as Yellich drove the police car up the winding front drive. The garden, too, he noticed, was equally expansive, wide lawns, landscaped rockeries, a pond. Yellich parked the police car behind a blue BMW. Hennessey and Yellich got out as the front door opened. A pale-skinned youth stood on the threshold, smiling as the police officers approached the house. 'You must be the police?'

'We are.'

'Bernard told me to be on the look out for you. Please come in.' He stepped aside.

Hennessey and Yellich stepped into the house, entering a large square hallway at the side of which was a wide, angular stairway. The youth knocked on a door to the left of the hallway, tapping softly, reverently. There was an over-extended utterly imperious pause, so Hennessey would long remember, and after a full sixty seconds had elapsed the pale-skinned youth showed no sign of knocking again, and in fact showed every sign of enjoying the game that was clearly been played. Hennessey had to fight the urge to push the door open. But then, as if knowing just how far to go, before any confrontation was unavoidable, a voice from within the room said 'come'.

Hennessey and Yellich entered the room which, as expected, was wide and spacious and which employed a vast sheet of glass as a window to give a further impression of space. The room was an office, a desk, shelves of textbooks, a filing cabinet beyond the desk. Two easy chairs stood beside a low coffee table. The man in the room, the man who had waited arrogantly in excess of a minute before responding to the knock was a large man, very large, broad of shoulder, completely filling out the chair in which he was sitting. The man was Bernard Ffyrst and Hennessey thought, please turn around Mr Ffyrst, please turn round so my good sergeant here and I can see your deeply scratched face.

'It's the police, Bernard,' the youth spoke. He had a local accent and a manner of speaking which didn't convey the impression of an education.

'I thought it would be.' Bernard Ffyrst's voice was calm, controlled, soft, learned. Still he did not turn round, but continued writing.

Avoiding.

Hennessey suddenly realised the pause, the refusal to turn to face his visitors were avoidance techniques. He knew he was no psychologist, but he was a career police officer close to retirement. To all intents and purposes, the only other job he had ever done was two years National Service in the Royal Navy. He'd been a police officer for in excess of thirty years, he was a student of human behaviour and this man, seated, refusing to turn to face them was a man who was avoiding the police, and who avoids the police but those who are guilty? It was then, just then, in this aloof, distant from the road house of unashamed, conspicuous consumption, in this lifestyle which was far, far, beyond the means of most mortals, that Hennessey knew, just knew, that Bernard Ffyrst was the man who had murdered Norris Smith many years ago. He also remembered the wisdom of Yellich's observation, the observation about the lengths a man would go to, to preserve his lifestyle at such a critical age in life. He was a barrister, in his forties, probably about to take silk, if he hadn't already done so, a golden, golden road ahead of him, of wealth, even more than he enjoyed at present, and great status in the community. In terms of motivation then, he could also be linked to the murder of Margaret South. Little wonder he turned away when two police officers, casting long shadows, called on him, at his house, in the study of his house.

Yellich, standing beside and a little way behind Hennessey also pondered the difference between Ffyrst senior and Ffyrst junior. Ffyrst senior, dominating his room in his firm's office in St Leonard's Place, where the heavy door shut out the bustle from the street and the hallway, was illuminated by a massive crystal chandelier. By contrast, Ffyrst junior, though large of frame, as bulky as his father, turned away from the officers in a gesture, Yellich thought, of subservience.

Then Bernard Ffyrst turned round. He was a heavy-jowled man, with a double chin, short hair. He was dressed casually in a large, very large T-shirt and lightweight summer slacks, but both officers thought he was a man who would be an intimidating presence in wig and robe in a senior court of law.

His face was smooth. Not the slightest trace of a scratch.

Both officers felt the other's disappointment.

'Leave us.' Ffyrst addressed the youth who

left the room, closing the door behind in a display of instantaneous obedience. Ffyrst looked at Hennessey, ignoring Yellich, but made no attempt to speak.

'Mr Ffyrst?' Hennessey broke the silence, and for the first time noticed Ffyrst's piercing eyes, coldly piercing eyes.

'That is I.' Ffyrst indicated the chairs beside the coffee table. 'Please take a seat, gentlemen, and please keep your voices down.' He indicated the door. Then said loudly. 'Go away, Matthew, I want to hear your feet in the hallway.' And Matthew's feet were duly heard, scampering away. 'He'll be back,' Ffyrst smiled. 'It's nice to have him and his other friends around the house, a man needs distractions, but they come at a price and one of the prices I pay is that I live with sets of ears that tend to glue themselves to doors. Now, gentlemen, how may I help you?'

'You were expecting us?' Hennessey sat as invited, Yellich did likewise.

'Well my chambers phoned me asking if they could give you my address upon production of an ID card. You must have looked me up in the business section of the telephone directory?'

'We did.'

'I'm ex-directory here, of course.'

'Of course.'

'But there's little point in having your business number ex-directory. So I gathered you'd call, no point in obtaining an address unless you intend to visit, I'd say. So, what can I do for you? If you'd be brief. I have work to prepare. I'm in court tomorrow, you see.'

'We won't detain you any longer than necessary, Mr Ffyrst.'

'You're too kind.' Outside the door a floor-board creaked. Ffyrst raised his eyebrows, smiled, then bellowed, 'Go away Matthew!' He turned to the officers. 'He likes me to get angry with him, you see. It's a game he plays. I think it makes him feel secure. I can cope with that. Once, you know, I had a young house guest who ... well, light-finger-ed isn't the phrase ... had to let him go. He's in Full Sutton now, doing five years for Grievous Bodily Harm. Wanted an old lady's pension, you see, said old lady felt disinclined to surrender said pension ... I think you can conjure the rest of the story. I was in court when he was sentenced, he didn't recognise me in my wig and gown. Probably wouldn't recognise me in clothes at all. But Matthew's games I can live with, accommodate even. But, I digress.'

'Yes ... Mr Ffyrst does the name South

mean anything to you? As a person's surname, I mean.'

'No. Can't say it does. No one in my social
circle, that's for certain, not a name of a
client that I can recall.'

'Margaret South?

'No.'

'How about Margaret Tennyson? Does
that name ring bells?'

'It does ... yes. Distant bells, but bells ring.
I was at university with a woman of that
name, daughter of a vicar.'

'A bishop,' Hennessey said slowly, gently.
'She was the daughter of a bishop.'

'Was...?'

'Was. She married and became Mrs Margaret South, wife of a doctor, a general practitioner in Harrogate.'

'Knaresborough,' Yellich corrected him,
'though the distance between the two towns
is trifling.'

'Knaresborough,' Hennessey repeated.

'Stayed local then. One or two of us did.'

'She was murdered last night.'

'Oh, my heavens!' Bernard Ffyrst's jaw
fell, quite noticeably, but not overdone. If it
was an act, and Hennessey felt certain that
it was, then it was an act which was not lost
in the overdoing. No ham here. 'Poor Margaret ... same age as me, forties, quite a

critical phase in life. If you haven't made a mess of it you begin to enjoy the returns on the investments you made in your twenties and thirties and have a realistic idea of what the next twenty years will bring. It's an unfair time to lose your life.'

'What time isn't?' Hennessey asked. 'Except perhaps after a reasonable innings and then by natural causes.'

'Well yes, we all must meet the ferryman ... but even so.'

'Can you tell us where you were last night, Mr Ffyrst?' Bernard Ffyrst's eyes narrowed, then he gasped and turned his eyes from Hennessey, then he looked at him again. 'Mr...? Sorry, I didn't catch your names.'

'We didn't give them. I am Chief Inspector Hennessey, this is Detective Sergeant Yellich.'

'Hennessey and Yellich.' Ffyrst repeated the names as if committing them to memory. 'You know gentlemen, I have not seen Margaret since graduation, in excess of twenty years ago. If you are suggesting that I have some connection with her murder, then I'd like you to make your suspicions plain, and I'd like you to do so now.'

'Just answer the question.'

A pause. An icy, piercing look, then. 'Here.'

'All evening?'

'All evening.'

'Alone?'

'No,' Ffyrst smiled. 'I had company.'

'Matthew?'

'I wish I could say, Mark, Luke and John as well, but I'm obliged to say Tommy and Eric. They're friends of Matthew's. We play-ed games all evening, we four.'

'I'll bet you did.'

'I'll let that disagreeable insinuation pass, Chief Inspector, but it's what is known in my line of work as an alibi.'

'I've come across the term.'

'Pretty well unbreakable one as well, I'd say.' Bernard Ffyrst looked not displeased with himself.

'We called on your father the other day.'

'It was you two gentlemen?' Ffyrst growl-ed, menacingly.

'Just me,' Yellich offered.

'I was curious, but not overly so. Police often call on solicitors, but not solicitors like my father, he doesn't do criminal work.'

'I gathered,' Yellich said. 'I visited his offices.'

'Gentlemen, I give you fair warning, I find your comments a little too personal, dis-tastefully so.'

'It was not meant disrespectfully, sir.'

'It was taken thusly.'

'In fact, the reason why we called on your father, Mr Ffyrst, links with the reason we have called upon you.'

'Oh...?' Ffyrst became guarded, noticeably so. Hennessey then realised, fully realised that if Bernard Ffyrst had been implicated in the murders of Norris Smith and Margaret South, that he was going to be a very difficult fish to land. He was not the sort of man to take a lure or swallow live bait.

'Well, if you knew Margaret South, née Tennyson, at university, you must also know of Norris Smith?' Hennessey held eye contact and saw what he was looking for; a flash of fear across the eyes of Bernard Ffyrst.

'Yes, I knew him.' Guarded, not giving anything away. 'I say ... Hennessey ... you're not related to Charles Hennessey, a barrister in the North Eastern circuit?'

'I'm his father.' Hennessey's chest swelled with pride.

'I don't know him well, chatted once, told me his father was a police officer, "he nicks 'em, we get 'em off" was his line.'

'Yes, he's said that to me, but let's not wander too far from the issue.'

'Of course.'

'Norris Smith's body was found recently.'

'So I read.'

'He too was murdered.'

'So I read.'

'His body was found buried in a shallow grave, in a shallow grave in a wood once owned by you.'

'No it wasn't. His body was found buried in a shallow grave in a wood once owned by my father. He sold it to raise capital for a housing venture ... but as to the location of the grave, again, so I read.'

'When did you last see Norris Smith?'

'Must have been at a party after finals. Everybody was there, don't remember him, though.'

'Did you murder Norris Smith?'

Ffyrst flushed with anger. 'What did you say? What did you say?' His voice echoed round the room, probably round the house as well. Matthew wouldn't have to have his ear pressed to the door to hear Ffyrst's explosion.

'I said, did you murder Norris Smith?' Hennessey spoke softly, pleased to see that if Bernard Ffyrst could not be lured, he could be provoked.

'That's not funny. Not remotely so.' The anger was quickly restrained. Ffyrst became guarded again, very cautious. But the eruption of anger had occurred, and Hennessey knew that such men can be made to trip themselves up.

'No, it's not, in fact I'm pleased we have some common ground, something we can share, if you like. We both believe the murder of Norris Smith is not funny. We both believe it's really quite serious.'

'So is that why you're here? Is that what you believe, that I murdered Norris Smith?' Ffyrst smiled. 'That's laughable. I mean, look what I've got.' He waved an arm as if inviting Hennessey and Yellich to look around his room. 'My status, my career; I knew that this was ahead of me, even at university. I knew what sort of lifestyle I was heading for. Do you think I'd throw all this away by murdering a harmless, helpless oik like little Norris Smith? That goofy little cretin from pie and peas and "kiss me quick" candyfloss land?'

'I have been a police officer pretty well all my working life, Mr Ffyrst, and I can tell you that people have taken life for reasons so petty that not even a ten-year-old would get into an argument about, and I can further tell you that what you have here is nothing, nothing compared to what I've seen people swap for a place in a cell for four with a piece of earthenware for them to share between them.'

Bernard Ffyrst fell silent, as if lost for words. But then, 'But not lawyers, none of them would be lawyers. A lawyer would know how difficult it is to get away with a crime. I'm a lawyer.'

'Is one way of looking at it, Mr Ffyrst.'

'And what on earth would be my motivation, I couldn't benefit from his death in any way at all?'

Hennessey nodded. 'And that is another way of looking at it.'

Ffyrst smiled, the balance of the argument was tipping in his favour, but his face fell when Hennessey said, as he stood. 'But a lawyer would know the importance of evidence, wouldn't he? A lawyer would know how to cover his tracks. Wouldn't he? A lawyer would also know how easy it is to get away with a crime. Wouldn't he?'

Bernard Ffyrst swivelled in his chair and turned back to his papers as Hennessey and Yellich left his office. In the hallway of the house, Matthew, with an annoying speaking voice confirmed that last night he 'n' a few others, and 'Bernard' spent the entire evening in the house.

The two officers sat in the car outside Bernard Ffyrst's house, leaving leisurely. In their own time.

'He's guilty, skipper.' Yellich turned the

ignition key and gunned the engine. 'Guilty as sin.'

'I know.' Hennessey stared straight ahead at the soft rolling landscape of green fields and isolated stands of trees, meadows containing contented sheep and cattle, at the vast wide blue sky. 'I know ... I know ... I know. But where do we go from here?'

'The Reverend James?' Yellich suggested.

Hennessey glanced at him.

'Well, skipper, you see it strikes me that twenty years ago something very significant happened in a group of recently graduated students of the university.'

'Being the murder of Norris Smith?'

'Right. Margaret South was a tortured soul in the last weeks of her life. She was on the verge of reporting something.'

'Which could only be the murder of Norris Smith?'

'So I believe. Bernard Ffyrst was defensive. He has some thing to hide.'

'Go on,' Hennessey smiled.

'There's only one link left for us.'

'Reverend Simon James?'

'Yes, Skipper. I know we've seen him twice already but we'll see him for as often as it takes. He is the only person in that group who'll co-operate with us. I don't know what we're going to ask him, but let's just wing it.'

'All right,' Hennessey nodded. 'Let's go and wing it.'

'Anyway,' Yellich engaged first gear and let in the clutch. 'It's a conspiracy, has to be, if Margaret South scratched the face of her murderer and Bernard Ffyrst's face is unscathed, somebody else's face isn't and that person might just be part of the same year group at the university as Ffyrst, Smith and South, née Tennyson.'

'And our only friendly link with that group, as you say, is the Reverend James.'

She hadn't been like the others. She hadn't folded quietly, she wanted to live, she had wanted to live all right, just wouldn't give up. The man felt his face. Sore, so sore ... those nails ... he couldn't go out like this, he'd have to stay in. He had enough to keep him going. But those nails...

Simon James looked at Hennessey, then at Yellich, and then back to Hennessey. They sat in the small study of the house which was neat and well ordered, in contrast to the shambolic interior of the rest of the vicarage. 'Margaret ... I can't believe it.'

'I'm afraid it's true, Reverend James. She put up quite a struggle and has left plentiful evidence which may identify her attacker if we can locate him. But robbery wasn't the motive, her jewellery wasn't removed and her body was found in a remote place.'

'And you say something was troubling her?'

'So it would seem. I'd be obliged if you'd keep this to yourself, Reverend, we are taking you into our confidence because you may be able to help us.'

'Of course. I appreciate your faith in me. Thank you. The inference is that she was troubled by the murder of Norris. That's what you're saying?'

'Yes. Her husband can offer no reason known to himself why she should be so troubled. Marriage was healthy, sufficient money, a marriage with a "no secrets" pact ... Dr South's impression was that she was troubled by an event deep in her past, some incident which took place before they married. Mrs South was a woman of integrity, so we have come to learn, and she resigned from the Harrogate Magistrates Bench without giving a reason.'

'So whatever was troubling her involved some degree of criminality. She'd done some deed, the memory of which she'd buried as people do if the deed is sufficiently awful, it had emerged years later and upon its re-emergence, she felt she could no longer sit as a magistrate? Is that the gist of your thinking?'

'Yes.'

'The awful event being the murder of Norris Smith?'

'Yes. We have met Bernard Ffyrst. He is cagey. Very defensive. But no marks on his face.'

'So Bernard murdered Norris?'

'So we believe.'

'Well...' Simon James glanced out of the window of his study at the lawn. 'Well, that's possible. It's possible in the sense that Bernard had such contempt for Norris that a spur of the moment explosion of violence would be possible. And if Margaret was present ... she may have gone along with it. You see Bernard had a way of making people do what he wanted them to do, and Margaret, I remember as a co-operative, accommodating soul. She could have been coerced or bullied or manipulated into doing something she would have cause to regret. I can see that.'

'Was Margaret particularly close to Bernard Ffyrst?'

'Not particularly, and certainly not ever did he and she comprise an "item". They were members of the same gang within the

251

year group, went out for a drink as a group, sat up late drinking coffee as a group, sat rolling drunk in the back of the Land Rover falling over each other.'

'The Land Rover?'

'Yes ... the not so originally named "Green Goddess" ex-military beast of a machine, belonged to a bloke called Paul Stapylton. We used to pile into it on Sunday evenings and drive out to the Falcon Bearer, it's a pub just outside York. It was the one place that was unique to our group. One of us discovered it, told the others, we visited it, kept it to ourselves, our little bolt hole from university life. It was quite easily accessible but we didn't want to turn it into another student-dominated pub, so we made a pact and kept mum about it. Every Sunday evening in the Falcon Bearer, that was the pattern.'

'Where is it?'

'Village called Poppleton St Mary. Out the posh end of York, beyond Poppleton itself, tucked away down a very minor road. Lovely village, lovely pub. I'd like to go and visit, just for nostalgia's sake. But we used to go there in Paul Stapylton's massive green Land Rover and Norris would drive us back. You see, that was Norris's place in the group, he stayed "dry" so the rest could drink and, in return, he'd get to drive the Goddess back to the university. That was some small compensation for him. He liked driving the thing, but he liked drinking more. So staying sober was a hard thing for him to do, but he was quite easily bullied into being the driver.' Simon James paused. 'Paul Stapylton's local, you know.'

'Is he?'

'Stapylton's Micro Engineering in the Business Park.'

'I've seen the sign on the factory from the road.'

'That's him. He took a good degree, didn't practise, disappeared into the woodwork then re-emerged as the proprietor of Stapylton Micro Engineering. There was an article about him in the *Post*. Started in a garage, now he's in "the Park" micro engineering, gadgets and gizmos that are essentially very simple, but are too small to see without a microscope.'

Driving back to York, Hennessey glanced out of the passenger side window and said, 'Rather interested in the Land Rover.'

'Occurred to me, too, boss.' Yellich kept his eyes on the road. 'Very handy for carrying a body across a field to a wood. Exactly what that machine is designed to do, carry persons, ideally alive and fighting fit, across fields. Chat with Mr Stapylton, skipper?'

Hennessey glanced at his watch. It was nearly six p.m. 'Tomorrow, Yellich, tomorrow.'

Eight

In which the net closes, and Michael Jolly is nice for perhaps the final time.

FRIDAY

The man was lying. Hennessey knew that.

It was the forced calm of the man.

It was the forced eye contact.

It was the give-away nervousness in the voice.

'Not since university days?' Hennessey repeated.

'As I said.' Stapylton sat behind his desk. Hennessey read the room, neat, ordered, everything in its place, a photograph of a Rolls Royce, of a yacht. Here was a man who liked things his way, and a man who liked possessions.

'She may have called herself Margaret South.'

'Tennyson, South ... it's the same Margaret. I'd know her, and I haven't seen the

255

woman in ... twenty years or more. I am a busy man, Chief Inspector.'

'We won't take up too much of your time, Mr Stapylton.'

'If you don't mind,' said testily. 'The company is on the verge of something big with a Japanese customer, you know how they like small things ... micro engineering has an appeal for them. I wouldn't want to lose the order.'

'We'll be away as soon as we can, Mr Stapylton.' Hennessey spoke softly. 'If you want us out, the sooner, the more you'd better co-operate.'

'I am co-operating.' Stapylton sat back in his hinged leather chair.

'Good, good. Now, having ascertained that you haven't seen Margaret South for twenty years, would you know what might be concerning her?'

'What sort of question is that?' Stapylton laughed. 'I mean, if I haven't seen Margaret for twenty years, how should I know what's on her mind now?'

'If whatever was on her mind was in connection with her university days. If something was plaguing her from her past, that part of her past that you have in common.'

'You're speaking in riddles, Inspector. Sorry, Chief Inspector. Why choose her university days? There's twenty years after that for anything to have happened in.'

'She was married straight from the degree ceremony, Mr Stapylton, successfully so. Her husband, who we find credible, informs us that Mrs South didn't do anything from the day of her wedding to the day of her death that she need feel guilty about, nothing at all, nor would she feel guilty about. It's highly unlikely that she did anything in her childhood, being the daughter of a bishop...'

'Being the daughter of a bishop wouldn't prevent you from doing something you'd rather folk didn't find out about.' Stapylton snapped the retort. He had, Hennessey noted, an unpleasant, short-tempered aspect to his personality.

'I was thinking of the lifestyle she would have led. At boarding school during term time, the bishop's residence during the holidays, grew up in that environment, the constraints, the expectations. That's our thinking ... unlikely, highly unlikely that she did anything before the age of eighteen that would cause her to feel obliged to resign as a magistrate when in her forties.'

'She did that?'

'She did that. As if haunted by something. So really, we are left with a three-year gap, being her university days. Then she was an adult, away from home, among undergraduates, after which she got married and had children. So her conduct prior to the start of university is, by implication and reasonable assumption, accounted for. Her conduct after she got married is vouched for by a man of credibility, to wit, her husband.'

'That just leaves the three years in between.' Yellich spoke for the first time since the interview commenced. 'The years that you and she shared as part of a larger group of people.'

'People such as Norris Smith.'

'Norris...' Stapylton gasped. 'Oh, Norris ... I haven't thought of him in years.'

'Haven't you?' Hennessey raised an eyebrow. 'Not even when the remains found at the beginning of this week were identified as his? Got quite a lot of publicity. You must have seen it, *Yorkshire Post*, *Calendar*, *Look North*, they all covered it, Radio York, the lot.'

'Well, apart from that ... not before this week. That's what I meant.'

'Ah, I see. So you have no idea what Margaret South, then Margaret Tennyson, might have been part of during her university days which would cause her so much

258

anguish now?'

'No,' said firmly.

'All right. Moving on.'

'How long is this going to take?'

'It'll take as long as it takes,' Hennessey said firmly.

'It's a murder inquiry,' Yellich added. 'Possibly a double murder.'

'A double murder ... who else...?'

'Norris Smith.' Hennessey sat forward.

'Norris...?'

'He was murdered.' Yellich remained still, motionless save for his jaw which moved only when he spoke. 'By having his head beaten in, massive skull fracture, death would have been instantaneous.'

'You see, that's our thinking,' Hennessey smiled. 'We have to knit it closer together before we can go to the CPS with it.'

'CPS?'

'Crown Prosecution Service.' Hennessey thought Stapylton was feigning ignorance but he indulged him anyway.

'Oh...'

'Sometimes known to the police canteen culture as the Criminal Protection Service, but we're confident that we can give them something that they can run with in this case.' Hennessey paused. 'You see, Norris Smith was murdered during the summer of the final exams. You and Mrs South knew him.'

'Yes.'

'His body was discovered on land, which at the time of the murder, was owned by a gentleman called Ffyrst.'

'Ffyrst?' Stapylton raised his eyebrows.

'Why, is that name significant to you? Do you know of anybody called Ffyrst?'

'I did. Bernard Ffyrst. He was part of that group.'

'Seen him recently?'

'No. As you see, I'm a businessman. I took a law degree, never practised. I imagine Bernard joined his father's firm.'

'He's a barrister.'

'Really? Good for him.'

'So you see, Mr Stapylton, it's our belief that Norris was murdered by his university … well, I hesitate to use the word "friends", but you know what I mean.'

'His peers.'

'A better word. I didn't benefit from an education.'

Stapylton didn't react.

'Norris Smith had few friends, according to his family, only the ones he made at university. He was murdered, then buried on land belonging to the father of one of his "peers", thank you for that word by the way,

I'll use it.'

'You're welcome.'

'Stranger murders are rare, usually a person is murdered by someone known to them.'

'So I have read.'

'When a murder victim is buried, it's pretty near cast-iron certainty that they were murdered by someone known to them. Further indicating that he was murdered by his ... peers, as you say.'

'No. You say. I offered only the word.'

'Yes,' Hennessey nodded. 'Victims of stranger murders are left lying in a pool of blood in the gutter while the perpetrator steals away into the shadows ... or die on the floor of a pub following a fight ... but buried, very unusual, few victims of stranger murders have ever been buried in shallow graves in my experience.'

'Nor mine.' Yellich continued to remain stiff, fixing Stapylton with a gimlet gaze, now in himself also convinced that the man was not being wholly truthful.

'So this is why we are here, Mr Stapylton. To see if you can shed any light on the matter.'

'Am I under any suspicion?'

'Should you be?'

'No.'

'Then you're not. Your name was given to us by another member of the group, Simon James.'

'Seb,' Stapylton smiled. 'What's he doing now?'

'He's a clergyman. Not as elevated as Margaret South's father was. A vicar, a minister in the Anglican church, out by Harrogate way.'

'Well, I never.' Stapylton shook his head. 'He was fairly wild at university, drank a lot, stood on tables ... but they do say that the wild ones will become the conservatives. Well, well, well. And he gave my name?'

'As one of the group who have remained local. If necessary, we'll trace all the group, using Interpol if we have to until we are certain that no one has evidence to offer in respect of Norris Smith's murder.'

'And if no evidence is forthcoming?'

'The case is shelved and will gather dust.'

The reply brought on an instant relaxing of Stapylton's manner. Then as if realising what he had betrayed, he said, 'That's a shame, I mean for Norris ... his family.'

'It's the way of it, Mr Stapylton. But the murder of Margaret South is a different matter. If Mrs South was linked to Norris Smith's death, as if she was about to give information about it, then the person who murdered her was also linked to his death in some way, but also lives locally.'

'Could have come a long way to silence her. Nowhere in the developed world is less than twenty-four hours distant from any other place in the developed world.'

'We think local.'

'Why?'

'Why do you ask?'

'No reason, just curious.'

'There's only three people still alive from that year group who live locally: Bernard Ffyrst, your good self and Simon James. The latter was proven to be overseas when Norris Smith was murdered. If Margaret South was agonising about what to do, if, if she had some involvement with Norris's murder, we feel it's likely that she may have contacted someone else who had some involvement with the murder. And if that person sought to silence her by murdering her, and her murder has a local feel to it...'

'Am I under suspicion?'

'No,' Hennessey smiled. 'Believe me, no finger of suspicion points to you. Your face isn't scratched. No point in asking you for a DNA sample.' Stapylton looked curiously at Hennessey and then at Yellich.

'Margaret South fought violently for her life. She badly gouged the face of the person who murdered her.'

'Blood under each one of her fingernails,' Yellich added.

'Can't hide damage like that, and we'll find it. When we do, we've got the killer.' Hennessey stood. Yellich did the same. 'We'll let ourselves out.'

Stapylton's face drained of colour.

In the grounds of Stapylton Micro Engineering, Hennessey and Yellich pondered the cars. A gleaming maroon Rolls Royce caught their eye. 'Run a registration check on yon.' Hennessey pointed to the car.

The results of the registration check was radioed to them while they drove back to Micklegate Bar Police Station. It was registered to Mrs Stapylton of 'The Pastures', Tollingbeck, Wetherby.

'It's his,' said Hennessey. 'The house and car are in her name in case the business collapses. What did you think of him?'

'Quite a lot. None of it good,' Yellich replied as he slowed the car for a pelican crossing. 'A man with something to hide.'

'Lying through his teeth, if you ask me,' Hennessey growled as he watched an old lady with a shopping trolley negotiate the crossing.

Hennessey wrote up the visit to Paul

Stapylton, recorded his suspicions that the man had something to hide, then he placed his pen down and glanced at the wall. A possibility occurred to him. The more he thought about it, the more it became a probability. He stood, reached for his jacket and went down the CID corridor to Yellich's office. Yellich sat at his desk hunched over a pile of files. He glanced up as Hennessey stood in the door frame of his office.

'Busy?' asked Hennessey.

'Paperwork, skipper.'

'I see. What are you doing for lunch?'

'Lunch? Canteen I suppose, skipper, subsidised food, bearable and cheap.'

'Cheap I grant you, but bearable...' Hennessey grimaced. 'Look, if you were to meet an old university friend after twenty years, where would you choose as a rendezvous? I don't mean where specifically, I mean what sort of place?'

'Well,' Yellich leaned back in his chair. 'Somewhere mutually convenient, somewhere easily accessible...'

'Yes. What about somewhere you used to frequent? A specific place that had significance for you when you saw a lot of each other?'

'Like the pub the gang used to go to on a Sunday evening to escape the university, you mean?'

Hennessey smiled. 'Just what I was thinking, Yellich. Grab your coat, let's go and see if the Falcon Bearer does pub lunches. And bring the photograph of Margaret South from the mis per file.'

'Well I didn't see her, either alone or with someone.'

Hennessey felt a twinge of disappointment, but he had by means of compensation found the Falcon Bearer, at Poppleton St Mary, as pleasant a pub as you could find. Tastefully decorated, an impressive cellar of real ales, lunches and dinners. A place to bring Louise D'Acre on one of their rare evenings out.

'I'll ask Sara,' the waiter added, 'she has a remarkable eye for detail and an amazing memory. Meanwhile would you care to order, gentlemen?'

'Not yet, thank you,' Hennessey smiled.

Sara revealed herself to be a svelte young woman, willow-like figure, graceful in a long cotton skirt with a floral pattern. A blue T-shirt and shoulder-length blond hair topped a face of angular beauty. She pondered the photograph and said 'yes'.

'Yes?'

'Yes. This lady was in here a day or two

ago. It's Friday today ... it was Tuesday. Yes, Tuesday lunchtime, they sat at that table in the corner.'

'They?'

'She and a gentleman, very well dressed, about the same age as her, forties ... I'd say. About my parents' age. I collected glasses from the adjacent table and overheard one, the man, saying that he'd "never been back to the wood".'

'Never been back to the wood.' Hennessey echoed and glanced at Yellich, who raised his eyebrows.

'Yes. I have excellent hearing. Deficient eyesight. I wear contacts, but my hearing is remarkable so I have found, able to hear things others cannot. I've made claims to hear things other people can't hear. They've disbelieved me, but I proved them wrong when the sound got louder. I don't think they knew I overheard them, they didn't believe I was close enough. But that's what he said all right. I didn't hear her response, I'm afraid.'

'The man, what did he look like?'

'Slim, very smartly dressed, casual but smart. Expensive watch.'

'Did they eat?'

'No. They only had a drink each. He drank beer, she drank a gin and tonic. Why, were

267

you hoping they bought a meal with a credit card?'

'Yes, actually,' Hennessey conceded.

'Remember their cars. She had a red Mercedes. We get them in here from time to time, but Rolls Royces, hardly ever.'

'A Rolls Royce?'

'A Silver Shadow. Quite an old model now but my boyfriend says they were the best car Rolls Royce ever made. A maroon one.'

'You'd recognise this man again?'

'Oh yes. Definitely. But you know your best bet?'

'No.'

'The CCTV tape. The manager has it covering the car park. We had a lot of thefts from cars, so he had it installed. It runs from opening to closing.'

'You don't say.'

In the manager's office, Hennessey and Yellich stood as the manager fast forwarded the tape from the previous Tuesday. A Rolls Royce swept into the car park, Paul Stapylton got out and walked towards the pub.

'There,' said Yellich.

The manager halted the tape.

'No, keep going, please,' Hennessey asked. 'We've got to catch them together on film.'

The manager forwarded the tape, people and cars hurried across a snowy screen.

268

Then Stapylton and Margaret South walked out of the pub.

'Normal speed, please,' Hennessey asked and the manager dutifully pressed a button on the handheld control. The officers watched as Margaret South and Paul Stapylton walked to their cars, halted, faced each other, talked, and then walked to Margaret South's Mercedes, got in and drove away together.

'Can we have the tape?' Hennessey asked. 'I'll give you a receipt.'

'Certainly.' The manager, a well-built man with a publican's attitude, friendly, with a short fuse, so thought Hennessey, ejected the tape, put it into its sleeve and handed it to him.

'Thanks, shouldn't tell you this, but just this morning that fella swore blind that the last time he saw that lady was twenty years ago.'

'Island amnesia, I think it's called.' The publican laughed as he switched off the video recorder and the television. 'I get it in here from time to time. Give a customer his bill, comes on with this, "We didn't eat all that" sketch. "Oh, but you did, sir. Oh, but you did".'

Johnny Fuller saw the van. It was 'new' in

the area. He copied the registration number in his notebook and, just for good measure, copied the writing on the side of the van as well.

Hennessey and Yellich stood looking at each other.

'Wonders of modern technology,' Hennessey smiled.

The two constables stood beside their pigeonholes, looking one after the other at the 'result' from Wetherby. The deoxyribonucleic acid test on the blood samples taken from beneath the fingernails of Margaret South's corpse belonged to Sean Knapper, aka, 'Suicide Pilot', aka 'Wild Man'. Thirty-five years old. He had an address in Holgate, behind the railway station, that part of York the tourists don't visit.

Sean Knapper sat is his chair. He didn't respond when the police officers opened his front door shouting his name. He didn't respond when they entered his living-room. He showed no reaction as the junior constable winced and sneered at his living conditions: the empty super lager cans, the silver foil that had once clearly contained illicit substances, the clothes strewn and abandoned among the newsprint and empty carryout cartons from the Chinese takeaway at the corner of the street.

Hennessey followed the constables and looked at Sean 'Wild Man' Knapper, Sean 'Suicide Pilot' Knapper, the mop of blond hair, the unwashed clothes, the cheap denims which betrayed thin legs, the ruddy face deeply, deeply gouged with angry linear marks where a woman, a few hours earlier, had violently, hopelessly, fought for her life. And the flies, already a dozen or so in number, a hot day, an open window. It never failed to amaze Hennessey just how rapidly musca domestica can find dead flesh.

'Not long,' Hennessey glanced at Yellich. 'Blood on the chair still looks tacky.'

'Must have just happened.' Yellich looked down at the corpse. 'No sign of forced entry, he knew his attacker, the door was closed but unlocked when we arrived. The attacker just closed the door behind him. Can't have missed him by more than half an hour. If that.'

'All right.' Hennessey addressed two constables and Yellich. 'This is a crime scene so we'll leave carefully, don't touch anything if you can help it.' The officers turned and retraced their steps into the hallway, into the street. Hennessey posted one constable at

271

the door of Sean Knapper's house, the other constable and Yellich he asked to commence house to house inquiries. 'Take one side of the street each, please.' While he returned to the area car, picked up the radio and requested the attendance of the police surgeon and the scene of crimes officers.

'Don't miss much, son.' Connie Kerr sat at the window. Yellich read her home, neat, clean, air freshener heavy in the room. 'I watch the street since my man died. It's all I do, watch our street, who comes, who goes. Better than television. Not much I don't notice, and Sean, Mad Sean, so he's dead. Aye ... well.'

'How do you know he's dead?'

'Because there wouldn't be a police officer standing at his door, and you and the other constable wouldn't be knocking on folks' doors, going along both sides of the street. That means he's been done in. Had to happen.'

'Why, was he a bad neighbour?'

'Wasn't. Kept quiet, kept himself to himself. He liked to drink. Oh yes, he liked his drink and a few other things I shouldn't wonder, but he liked his drink most of all. Didn't have to go into his home, just by looking at him you could guess what his

house was like. A refuse tip, I shouldn't
wonder.'

'Not for me to say, Mrs Kerr.'

'But I'm not far off the mark, am I?'

'Perhaps not.'

'He wasn't popular in the street, but he
wasn't the neighbour from hell either. Kept
strange hours. I'd be lying in my bed and I'd
hear a door open and shut and think that's
either Sean coming home or going out, two,
three, four a.m. But not any more, I dare
say. But he wasn't long for this world, you
could tell, I could tell. I'm right about most
things like that.'

'Did you see anything today?'

'A lot, but nothing to do with Sean. I sit at
my perch, here at nine o'clock each morning, until I go to my bed, except when I'm
in my little kitchen, making a meal or eating
a meal, or when I'm out shopping. Otherwise I'm here.'

'Did you go out today?'

'From about eleven o'clock till five minutes before the police arrived. Heard Sean
come home last night. So if he left his house
today, or someone visited him, it would have
been between eleven a.m. and the time
you arrived.' Yellich smiled and nodded.
'Thanks, that helps us a lot, Mrs Kerr.'

'Tell you who you could try.'

'Oh, yes?'

'Number fifteen, far end of the street, Mrs Fuller. She lives with her son, a young lad, poor soul, he's a penny short of a shilling. She's waiting for a place in a special school for him, but since he's learned to tell his numbers he's forever running up and down these streets writing down car number plates, but only the ones that have parked, the moving cars are going too fast for him, poor soul.'

Yellich beamed at her.

Johnny Fuller was pleased to show DS Yellich his list of numbers for that day. Yellich scanned the numbers and said, 'Tell me about this one, Johnny.'

'White van?' said Johnny Fuller, ten years of age, tall and lanky. He stood amid brightly coloured plastic toys and colouring books.

'Good. You wrote something beside the numbers?'

'The education people,' his mother said, 'they suggested he practise his letters when he can, so I suggested he wrote the wording on the side of delivery vans. He's safe to let out, he's got road sense.'

'I know, Mrs Fuller,' Yellich smiled at her. 'My own son is like Johnny, he's got special needs, too.'

Mrs Fuller blushed with relief. 'They're capable of more than folk credit them with.'

'Oh, I know. My son will be able to live semi-independently, so we hope. Johnny will really thrive once he's in school, the staff are dedicated. Whatever is in him, they'll get it out, and they'll do it with positive encouragement. He'll probably go to the school my son's in, Alma Road.'

'He's down for that school.'

'Had to be really, it's the only one in York.'

'We've just moved, not long in this house, that's why he's at home today.'

'Fortunate for us he is.' Yellich turned to the young boy. 'Now, Johnny, those letters ... do you know what they say?'

Johnny Fuller shook his head.

'But you copied them down exactly as they were on the side of the white van?'

Johnny nodded his head vigorously.

'And you copied them down today?'

Another vigorous nod of the head.

Yellich glanced at Mrs Fuller for confirmation.

'Yes, those are today's numbers. A new pad, you see, I bought him that pad when we were at the shops this morning, didn't I, Johnny?'

Johnny nodded his head.

'Then he went out collecting car numbers.'

'What time was that?'

'About eleven this morning. He came in for his lunch about twelve.'

'Can I keep this pad?'

'Well, yes ... yes.'

'The numbers are significant. There's been an incident further down the street.'

'I saw the police cars.'

'I'll pay for it.' Yellich took out his wallet and handed Mrs Fuller a five pound note.

'It didn't cost that much.'

'Buy Johnny something with the change.'

Yellich returned to Sean Kapper's house. A flash of a camera told him SOCO had arrived. As he was about to enter the house, the imposing bulk of Chief Inspector Hennessey stepped on to the pavement.

'Gold dust.' Yellich held up Johnny Fuller's notebook. He told Hennessey about the young lad, then turned the notebook so that Hennessey could read what he had written that morning. 'Look what he wrote beside the numbers, he said was the registration of what he described as a white van.'

'Stapylton Micro Engineering,' Hennessey said softly. 'Why am I not surprised, Yellich?'

Yellich shrugged. 'Confess, it didn't surprise me either, skipper. What have you got there.'

Hennessey held up a production bag, the self-sealing cellophane sachet contained a mobile phone. 'Can't see Kapper owning one of these, can you?'

'No. But I can see him taking it for himself, after he strangled the owner, especially if she put up a fight.'

'So can I, Yellich, so can I. And one of the last numbers phoned to or from that brain fryer will be Paul Stapylton's home or office.'

'Time we had a chat with Mr Stapylton, don't you think, skipper?'

'I think so. Lunch first, though. Hate to rush things. And I don't think he'll be going anywhere.'

DS Yellich found the tension in the interview room almost unbearable. And he was not under suspicion. He could only imagine what Paul Stapylton felt despite his calm exterior. The twin spools of the recording machine spun slowly, the red recording light glowed.

'I am Detective Chief Inspector Hennessey. The place is Micklegate Bar Police Station in the city of York. The time is...' he consulted his watch. 'Fourteen thirty-three on Friday, seventeenth of May. I am going to ask the other persons in the room to identify themselves.'

'DS Yellich.'

'Paul Stapylton.'

'Geraldine De Witt, of Cairncross & Co, Solicitors, High Petergate, York.' De Witt sat back, kept her eyes fixed on the table, her mind, so thought Yellich, was utterly fixed, utterly focused. She was a young woman – he thought her about twenty-five, grey suit, rocks and bangles. She had a notepad in front of her, a gold pen beside it. Like Ffyrst, Tend & Byrd, Yellich found time to ponder, Cairncross & Co, can clearly survive without Legal Aid work.

'Right...' Hennessey leaned forwards and clasped his hands in front of him on the table. 'Mr Stapylton,' Hennessey smiled. 'We meet again, and on the same day, too.'

'Yes.'

'Good. For the record, it is true that myself and my good sergeant here called on you this morning at your office, your business premises this morning?'

'Yes.'

'During that conversation you indicated that you had not seen Margaret South, née Tennyson, for in excess of twenty years, not since the party to celebrate your final

278

exams. Do you still maintain that fact?'

'I do.'

'Very well,' Hennessey paused. 'We'll leave that for the moment.' Paul Stapylton visibly relaxed and smiled. Hennessey didn't comment. He wanted Stapylton to lower his guard.

'Can you tell us where you were today between eleven a.m. and twelve p.m. midday?'

'At work.'

'Do you have a witness?'

'I dare say my secretary will tell you I was in the office.'

'She may have to. On oath.'

A pause. Stapylton glanced at Hennessey. 'I may have taken an early lunch.'

'How early?'

'I can't remember.'

'You can't remember,' Hennessey smiled. 'That is a comical answer. We are now only two and a half hours after midday and you can't remember if you had an early lunch or not?'

'Yes, I had an early lunch.'

'Where?'

'In town.'

'Where?'

'A pub, I saw one that advertised bar lunches so I went in.'

'Did you drive into York?'

'Yes.'

'In your car?'

'No, it's being serviced. I used one of the company vans.'

'How many vans does your company have?'

'Two.'

'Both of them in York today?'

'No. One is being used to collect some material from London.'

'I see, so only one van in York this day belonging to your company.'

'Yes. But London is only a three hours' drive away, the collection point is a small company in North London, very north London, the second van may be back by now, he got off early this forenoon.'

'But at eleven a.m. there was only one van in York belonging to your company?'

'Yes.'

'And you drove it?'

'Yes.'

'All right. Now to change tack again, do you know a man by the name of Sean Kapper, also known as "Suicide Pilot", also known as "Wild Sean"?'

'I don't.'

'Sure?'

'Positive.'

'I see. Now, what do you know of the murder of Norris Smith – he was a peer of yours at university? He was murdered in the summer after your final exams.'

'Nothing. I know nothing of his murder.'

'Sure?'

'Positive.'

'And of the murder of Margaret South?'

'Nothing.'

'Sure?'

'Yes. Yes.'

'My client has made his position quite clear, Mr Hennessey.'

'Yes.' George Hennessey relaxed. 'Mr Stapylton, did you arrange for Sean Kapper to murder Margaret South because Mrs South was about to give information to the police about the murder of Norris Smith, information which would have incriminated you, and one other person, namely Bernard Ffyrst?'

'Ffyrst...?' Geraldine De Witt spoke inadvertently and then fell silent.

For the benefit of Miss De Witt's curiosity and professional concern, he added, 'Bernard Ffyrst, barrister, son of Aaron Ffyrst of Ffyrst, Tend & Byrd, St Leonard's Place, York.'

'Yes, I know Bernard Ffyrst. He was a contemporary of ours, as you say. He and

281

Norris and Margaret and me and about thirty others.' Stapylton said as Geraldine De Witt put her hand to her forehead in a gesture of despair.

'Any recent contact with him?'

'No.'

'I see.' Hennessey paused. 'Right, I want you to listen to me, Mr Stapylton, just listen, and when I have finished speaking, myself and Sergeant Yellich here will leave you to discuss your options with Miss De Witt.'

Stapylton nodded slowly.

'Now, you have lied to us on a number of points, provenly so. You lied to me and my sergeant here, and you have repeated those lies in this interview which you know is being tape-recorded and so said lies are now a matter of record. We know that far from not seeing Margaret South for in excess of twenty years, you met in the Falcon Bearer pub in Poppleton St Mary on the Tuesday of this week, about midday, we have you on film. The landlord monitors the car park with CCTV. There is footage of you and Margaret South walking from the pub side by side, you stop, you talk and you both drive away in her car, leaving your Rolls Royce safely in the car park. In the pub, the young girl who does her work during the day in the pub remembers you and Margaret South sitting together, you were noticed because of the distinctive cars you both drove and as she passed your table she heard you say, "Never been back to the wood." Now Norris Smith was buried in a wood, a wood that belonged to Bernard Ffyrst's father at the time Norris Smith was murdered. You, Bernard, Norris, Margaret, all peers at university, same course year ... What other wood would you and Margaret South have had in common that you could refer to as "the" wood when speaking to her, other than the wood Norris Smith was buried in twenty-odd years ago?'

Stapylton's head sank forward.

'And today Sean Kapper was murdered. His face was badly gouged, his blood was found under Margaret South's fingernails, rapidly matched with our DNA database. Did you know he had a conviction for rape?'

'No...'

'Well, he had, so he was rapidly traced. We went to arrest him, found him deceased, no sign of a break-in so he knew his attacker. Probably turned his back on his attacker, inviting ye olde blunte object upon his head with great force whereupon said attacker fled. He was not seen, but his vehicle may have been. A little boy with limited faculties

283

practises his numbers by noting car registrations in a notebook. Sometimes he practises his letters by writing signs on the side of motor vehicles, and today on the first page of a notepad which was purchased this morning, between the hours of eleven and midday, he wrote the registration number of a van he hadn't seen before which was parked in the vicinity of Sean Kapper's house. The little boy lives on the same street as Sean Kapper. I should tell you, but I don't need to tell you what was written on the side of the van, do I, Mr Stapylton? And since you have just admitted driving the only one of your vans to be in York today for an "early lunch" in town, that places you perilously close to the murder scene. Another lie you see. You were not in a pub in the city having a bar meal, you were in Holgate. And you were in Holgate to murder Sean Kapper because we had just told you that the person who murdered Margaret South had a badly gouged face, and you got to him before we could so as to silence him.'

Geraldine De Witt looked at Paul Stapylton. The look said it all, it was a look which said, 'I can't help you'.

Hennessey saw the look and seized the moment. 'You have a choice, Paul. From this point on you either work for yourself or you work against yourself. Our scene of crimes officers are still at Sean Kapper's house, if we find just one fingerprint, one fibre that links to you, that'll put you right at the murder scene. We've also got Margaret South's mobile.'

Paul Stapylton looked up at Hennessey.

'Why do you look like that? Did you tell him to get rid of everything?'

No reply.

'No matter, but it's Margaret South's mobile and the last number she dialled on the day she died, the day she was murdered, was Stapylton Micro Engineering. She was contacting you, Paul. And she was contacting you to tell you that she was going to the police about Norris Smith's murder.' Hennessey paused. 'The time is fifteen thirteen hours. The interview is suspended to allow Mr Stapylton to consult with his legal adviser.' Hennessey switched off the tape recorder. He and Yellich stood and left the room. As he reached the threshold, Hennessey turned and said, 'I'll have refreshments brought in.' Geraldine De Witt nodded her thanks.

In the corridor, Yellich and Hennessey stood beside the coffee vending machine.

'It's still not all there, skipper.'

'I know,' Hennessey grimaced. 'Without a

285

confession the CPS won't run with it. Even if we can place Stapylton at the scene of Kapper's murder, it doesn't prove he did it. We might have to let that go, "leave it on file", as the expression has it. Maybe he'll cough when his conscience gets the better of him.'

'He's a lawyer, skipper, he'll cough to nowt.' Yellich sipped his coffee. 'And he's got another lawyer in there, advising him to cough to nowt.'

'So close. So close.'

'And another lawyer as a partner in crime. It gets worse.'

Geraldine De Witt stepped into the corridor. She looked at Hennessey and Yellich who stood fifteen feet away from the door to the interview room. 'Can my client have a word with you, please?'

Hennessey and Yellich glanced at each other and then placed their half-drunk plastic beakers of coffee on top of the vending machine and walked into the interview room. Hennessey reached for the on/off switch of the tape recorder.

'Off the record,' Geraldine De Witt said firmly.

Hennessey paused then switched the tape recorder on. 'Nothing's off the record.' He sat down, announced the time, asked the persons present to identify themselves and then said, 'I gather you wish to make a statement, Mr Stapylton?'

'I didn't say that,' Geraldine De Witt snapped.

'So, what do you want to say?'

'Since you insist on it being by the book, Chief Inspector, my client denies any knowledge of the murder of Norris Smith or of the unlawful disposal of his body. My client admits to seeing Margaret South. They were having an affair.'

Hennessey gasped. 'You'd sully the reputation of a woman like Margaret South?'

'But no knowledge of her murder. My client was in the house of Sean Kapper but found the gentleman already deceased and fled rather than become involved. My client has not see Bernard Ffyrst since university days.'

The silence lasted twenty seconds. It was broken by Geraldine De Witt who said, 'The burden of proof lies with you, Chief Inspector.'

'So I am aware, Miss De Witt.' Hennessey turned to Stapylton. 'What happened is that you and Margaret South and Bernard Ffyrst were implicated in the murder of Norris Smith. After twenty years Margaret South's guilt became so great that she was going to give herself up. You and Ffyrst couldn't persuade her not to, so you had her murdered.'

No reaction.

'You know what I further think, Mr Stapylton? I further think that of the three of you, you and Margaret South were the least involved, probably only helping to dispose of the body, bad enough, but you could have argued you acted in panic ... negotiated a reduced sentence. That's why Margaret South contacted you and not Bernard Ffyrst. She saw you as an ally.'

No reaction.

'Then when you realised Sean Kapper could be identified as her murderer, you murdered him to prevent him fingering you.'

No reaction.

'You know the irony of all this, Mr Stapylton? The irony is that if I am right, if you and Margaret South were minor players in the murder of Norris Smith, we would not have charged you in return for a statement implicating Bernard Ffyrst.'

Stapylton's jaw sagged. 'You would have done that?'

'Be careful what you say,' Geraldine De Witt said softly, but forcefully.

'Yes, we would have done that. The CPS would have agreed to that. Margaret would have lived to see her children thrive into adulthood and you would have carried on to make your fortune and the case would have been closed.'

Stapylton hung his head in his hands.

'Don't say anything.' De Witt warned again.

'But now it's too late. Margaret won't see her children grow to adults, and you may just make your fortune, but each day, each hour, you'll fear a police officer knocking on your door. Because I know what you did, you know what you did, and the case files on the murders of Norris Smith, Margaret South and Scan Kapper will never be closed, and the finger of suspicion points to you and Bernard Ffyrst. It needs just one slip of the tongue, one microscopic piece of evidence, one person coming forward to give evidence he or she has been withholding for whatever reason, and you are looking at three life sentences. You and Bernard Ffyrst. You can't imagine the sleepless nights that are ahead of you.'

Stapylton looked close to breaking. He breathed deeply.

'Your conscience eats you away from the inside, like a maggot eating an apple, it's relentless, and that not knowing who's at the door each time it's knocked on. Each time the phone rings you'll wonder if it's the police inviting you to the station so as to avoid the embarrassment of being collected from your work place or your home. Tomorrow, next month, next year, it'll never let up, and the older you get, the worse it gets ... ponder going down for three life sentences when you're fifty, sixty. That would be quite some drop from your lifestyle. At that age it's heart attack country: gaol for life in your fifties is a death sentence no matter how you look at it.'

'This is intimidation,' De Witt spoke strongly.

'No, it's not, it's advice, it's reality therapy. All will fall on you because of Bernard Ffyrst. You can't stand up to people like that, they have a way of controlling you, making you do things you don't want to do.'

'Yes ... he's like that...'

'Be careful,' De Witt hissed.

'You can't say no to him...'

'I've met people like that, once or twice ... you lose control of your mind, they can take over ... make you do things you know are wrong, but you do them anyway.'

Stapylton nodded.

'How much is your factory worth, Mr Stapylton?' Hennessey asked. 'If you sell it ... put the proceeds into a high-yield account.'

Stapylton glanced at him.

'Just helping you find a way forward. A statement now, depending on its content, you could be a free man in ten years, probably less. You'll have something substantial to come out to ... if you sell it, that big order from Japan you mentioned...'

'Yes...'

'So, do you want to sleep at night?'

'Sean Kapper ... that was self-defence. It was. I went there to offer him money to leave York for a week or two, just till his face healed over ... he became angry, said I wanted rid of him, saw it as a rejection ... he's touchy like that.'

'He was.' Hennessey didn't believe a word of Stapylton's confession, but he let the man talk, he was getting where he wanted to go, he was on his way to a very nice result, a very nice result indeed. 'He was touchy. As of this forenoon he's no longer "is" he's a "was".'

'Came at me with a knife. Hit him. Self-defence. Went down and hit his head.'

'On the back of a chair?'

'I lifted him up and put him there.' Said quickly, hurriedly.

'He was a big man. You lifted him all by yourself?'

'Yes.' Stapylton began to recover. 'Yes. All by myself.'

'How did you know Sean Kapper?'

'He...' Stapylton paused. 'Just knew him.'

'Right, Margaret South's murder. Bernard Ffyrst's idea?'

'Yes,' Stapylton nodded. 'I tried to persuade Margaret to let it lie, wouldn't do any good after this length of time ... she was all for going to the Law. Bernard wouldn't have it. He's a barrister, wants to be a judge, even being implicated in something like this would finish him.'

Yes, this was good, this was very good. 'And you had a lot to lose as well?'

Geraldine DeWitt sat expressionless, staring at the brown walls of the interview room. If her client wanted to bury himself, he could. She would still get her fee.

'But I could realise my assets if I had to, like you indicated. Sell up. I could sell it all for two, three million, put it all in a high-yield account, I'd have something to come out to. But Bernard, he'd come out to nothing. His house, all those cottages knocked into one, it's still heavily mortgaged. He was desperate. Had me pay Sean Kapper to murder her.'

'Where?'

'At Bernard's house.'

'Any witnesses?'

'Bernard's friend.'

'Matthew?'

Stapylton nodded.

'For the benefit of the microphone, please.'

A sudden look of shock ran across Stapylton's eyes as if he had forgotten about the silently spinning spools. He glanced quickly at Geraldine De Witt who kept her head facing forwards. Then he said, 'Yes, Matthew, Matthew Parr by name. He didn't see the murder, no one did, but Margaret was shown into a room where Sean and only Sean was waiting, and after a scream and crashing of furniture, only Sean emerged. Doesn't take a rocket scientist to work out what happened.'

'You provided Sean?'

'Yes. But I didn't do the murder.'

'Sean did.'

'On your say so.'

'Well...'

'You paid him?'

'Yes.'

'To murder Margaret South?'

'What else...'

'Yes or no?'

'Yes, yes, yes. What else were we to do? She was going to ruin both of us.'

'So you murdered her? Then what?'

'We put her body in a van, one of mine, the one that's on its way back from London right now.'

'We?'

'Me and Sean and Bernard.'

'Not Matthew Parr?'

'No ... He'd taken fright and was off like a spring hare.'

Hennessey and Yellich glanced at each other. An independent witness. Gold dust.

'Then?'

'We waited till dark, drove out into the country, don't know where. Just drove. Left her propped up against a tree. Drove back, dropped Sean off at Holgate, took Bernard home. I drove *home.*'

'Cool as a cucumber?'

'Numb with shock. I haven't been party to a murder before.'

'Norris Smith? He was murdered.'

'I didn't see that. I was outside with the Goddess.'

'The Goddess?'

'My Land Rover. We, me and Margaret and Bernard were sitting Bernard's parents house for a few weeks while they were in Barbados or some place, West Indies anyway. Just the three of us, lovely big old Victorian house. A really nice break after the pressure of finals, a summer in the country before the life's work began for us.'

'No Norris?'

'No. Bernard had it in for Norris from the word go. Huge domineering Bernard, little, shy, retiring Norris. Then, Bernard said he'd invited Norris to visit for the last two days of the holiday.'

'Surprising?'

'Surprised us. But Bernard said he thought we needed someone to laugh at.'

'To laugh at?' Hennessey echoed.

'It was the way Bernard thought. It was the way you thought in your twenties. He also said he wanted to show Norris what he was missing, in terms of lifestyle, Norris's parents—'

'Yes, we know Norris's background. Go on.'

'Well, on the last day, the day before Bernard's parents were to return, I was outside with the Goddess and I heard Margaret scream. I rushed into the house ... Norris was lying on the floor, bloody mass at the back of his skull. Bernard was standing behind the chair holding a golf club, blood on the golf club. Margaret was white, shaken ... again, you don't need to be a rocket scientist...'

'Then?'

'We just did what Bernard told us to do. Bundled Norris's body into the Goddess, buried him at night in a wood. Didn't know at the time the wood was owned by Bernard's family. That linked him to the murder. Not as bad as burying him under the patio, but it was a link.'

'Which we made.'

'Didn't you just. The next day Margaret and I drove into York. Didn't say a word, didn't speak, dropped her by the cholera burial ground outside the station. She got out and walked away. Never heard from her again until a few days ago. She was for reporting it. She'd buried the memory you see, then recovered it, and once she realised she wasn't remembering a dream—'

'Did she tell you what happened?'

'She said Bernard saw Norris's head sticking up above the back of the chair, he went away and returned with a golf club, and whack. He couldn't resist it, his contempt for Norris...' Stapylton sighed. 'That's how Margaret described it. She said Norris came back from the dead. She had a word for it, can't remember it now.'

'Well, you'll have plenty of time to rack your brains.'

'So how long will I get? Full co-operation, ten years you said? Out in five?'

296

'I made no promises. Certainly not before I heard your statement.'

Stapylton glanced at Geraldine De Witt. 'What am I looking at?'

'Twenty years. Out in fifteen. If you're lucky.' She picked up her notepad and gold-plated pen. 'I told you to remain silent. They couldn't have proved a thing.'

Stapylton paled.

'It was arranging the contract killing of Margaret South, and doing so in the presence of an independent witness, being Mr Ffyrst's ... friend. Any attempt to withdraw your statement now will be futile.' Geraldine De Witt stood. 'And when the police arrest Mr Ffyrst, as they doubtless will in a short time from now, and when he hears how you have implicated him, he will do as much as he can to implicate you. Just play with a straight bat and get your story in first.'

'You're leaving?'

'Yes. The De Witts are a long established legal family in the Vale of York, so are the Ffyrsts, our families are known socially and are linked distantly, but linked nonetheless, by marriage. I have therefore a conflict of interest. The police will provide a duty solicitor for you. Good day.'

Epilogue

The gracious reader, who has kindly read to the end of this tale, will doubtless be curious as to the fate of Bernard Ffyrst and Paul Stapylton. The gracious reader may also recall Michael Jolly whose grim discovery set the wheels of this story in motion.

Bernard Ffyrst stood impassively in the dock while the judge told him that he had brought disgrace upon the English Bar and upon a respected family who had for generations given much to the law. He was sentenced to two life sentences, for the murder of Norris Smith and for his part in the 'calculated' murder of Margaret South, and was ordered to serve a minimum of twenty years before being considered for parole.

Two years after that, Paul Stapylton also received a life sentence for the murder of Margaret South (he was not charged with the murder of Sean Kapper – the CPS ruling that there was insufficient evidence). He was visited in Durham gaol by his two sons. They were both bronzed after three weeks' holiday in Greece. They had returned to the family house to find a stranger living there, and his wife and his children and his dog and his cat. It transpired that the youthful Mrs Stapylton, in whose name was the high-yield account, the house, and contents therein, and also the cars, the Rolls Royce and her modest Volkswagen, had taken advantage of her stepsons' absence and sold up and left for places unknown with person or persons unknown. Paul Stapylton's sons asked him if he could let them have any money...

On the day that the jury at York Crown Court found unanimously against Bernard Ffyrst and Paul Stapylton, Michael Jolly was in traction in York City Hospital with both his arms and legs and ribcage in plaster. Not being able to sell his story to the media, he had tried again, during the trial so as to capitalise on the media attention. The media was quite happy to interview him but his story was not saleable. So he went to a pub to be nice to someone so that that someone would be nice to him, like his mother had long ago told him to do. He had been nice to a coal miner who had already been drinking for three hours by the time Michael Jolly sidled up to him with a 'hello' and a sickly smile. The man had been drinking because his girlfriend had left him, taking a large amount of money with her, and he really didn't need Michael Jolly to be nice to him – not just then.